Doctor Who — Castrovalva

This book is dedicated to M. C. Escher, whose drawings inspired it and provided its title. Thanks are also due to the Barbican Centre, London, England, where a working model of the disorienteering experiments provided valuable practical experience.

DOCTOR WHO
CASTROVALVA

Based on the BBC television serial by Christopher H. Bidmead by arrangement with the British Broadcasting Corporation

CHRISTOPHER H. BIDMEAD

Number 76
in the
Doctor Who Library

A TARGET BOOK

published by
the Paperback Division of
W. H. ALLEN & Co. Ltd

A Target Book
Published in 1983
by the Paperback Division of
W. H. Allen & Co. Ltd
A Howard & Wyndham Company
44 Hill Street, London W1X 8LB

First published in Great Britain by
W. H. Allen & Co. Ltd 1983
Reprinted 1984

Printed in Great Britain by
Hunt Barnard Printing Ltd, Aylesbury, Bucks.

ISBN 0 426 19326 1

CONTENTS

1

Escape from Earth

'He's changing,' said Adric. 'The Doctor's regenerating.'

A cold unfriendly morning had begun to whiten the sky beyond the high wire perimeter. Tegan exchanged a glance with Adric and Nyssa, but none of the three friends dared to approach the Doctor. For inside that red ocean of great-coat, festooned with the familiar long woollen scarf, the figure on the ground seemed so fragile as to be hardly there at all. They watched him struggle to sit up, and from that strangely smooth and vacant face they heard a voice that was not very like the Doctor's. But the sense of what he said was lost under the crisp intrusion of several pairs of footsteps running towards them across the tarmac.

The long pin-drop of silence shattered into confusion. In a moment uniformed guards loomed over them, and above the clamour of the approaching ambulance Tegan managed to hear: '. . . these are secure premises. You lot have got some explaining to do.'

As if you could explain something like that to an inquisitor behind the visor of a security helmet? You would have to retell the whole terrifying story of Logopolis, and of the Doctor's last deadly struggle with the Master—perhaps his last forever—high up there on the Pharos transmission tower in whose ominous shadow they now stood.

The guard took hold of her arm, none too gently, to steer her out of the path of the approaching ambulance, while his two colleagues closed in around Adric and Nyssa. Still shattered by the Doctor's terrible fall, Tegan turned her anger on the guards.

'Take your hands off me . . . This is an official uniform.' If she had a wild hope that they might somehow be impressed by her purple air-hostess outfit she was mistaken.

Adric's tone was more reasonable. 'Don't be silly,' said the boy, trying to sound calm. 'We want to help. But you can't take us away from the Doctor. Something may have gone wrong with his regeneration . . .'

The ambulance had drawn up beside them, like a white wall suddenly shutting them off from the Doctor. The driver jumped out and disappeared around the other side of the vehicle, and a man in a white coat emerged from the rear doors to follow him. The guards hustled the three companions against the side of the ambulance. 'Arms up and lean on it. Come on, quick.'

Swift professional hands searched Nyssa and Adric for weapons. As it came to Tegan's turn she noticed that by craning her head to the left she could look through the windows of the driving cab to the patch of ground on the other side where the white-coated man was bent over the Doctor. The uniformed driver had returned to fetch a stretcher from the back of the vehicle.

The guard concluded his search. 'No weapons.'

'Of course not,' Tegan snapped. 'We're all perfectly harmless . . . unfortunately.' Looking through the two windows of the driving compartment, she saw the ambulance men lifting the limp figure onto the stretcher. She closed her eyes tight, trying to shut out the reality of what was happening to the Doctor. After a fall from that height it seemed impossible that he should live at all. And yet just before the arrival of the guards they had all seen him open his eyes and reach out towards the shadows behind him where his future had been waiting. That surely must have been a dream, thought Tegan, remembering with a shudder the way the vague and luminous figure they had come to know as the Watcher had stepped out into the light, grasping the Doctor's hands and drawing closer and closer until their two shapes began to merge. This was the process Adric kept calling 'regeneration', a process that all the Lords of Gallifrey went through from time to time. Except that this time because of the apocalyptic events surrounding their adventure in Logopolis, the Doctor's new self had overlapped the old, watching and waiting for the

2

moment of union.

Adric was still trying to reason with their captors. 'The point of this Pharos Project of yours is to track down alien intelligences, isn't it? We thought we'd save you the trouble and come to you.'

He looked across at Nyssa for confirmation, and she shook the curls of her chestnut hair in a curt nod. It was unusual for Nyssa to tell anything but the strict truth, but in this case the strict truth was far too complicated. And it was perfectly true that they were alien intelligences.

The disbelieving guards peered back at them. Adric, with his strange smile and wicked black button eyes might well have passed for a visitor from another planet, for all the guards knew. And come to think of it, the younger of the two girls did have a remote, aristocratic quality that was somehow unEarthly. But the other girl's broad accent could never have come from anywhere further than the Antipodes.

'We're what you're looking for,' Adric repeated. He was starting to become heated now, forgetting to use a grown-up, reasonable tone of voice. 'Alien intelligences. I come from somewhere up there . . .' He jabbed his finger towards a distant spot in the sky with such emphasis that the guards couldn't resist looking up. 'That's the way into E-Space . . .'

The ambulance man in the white coat looked up too as he was on the point of climbing in after the stretcher. The hesitation was a mistake, because at that moment the engine sprang into life, and the vehicle suddenly began to accelerate across the enclosure with its unlatched rear doors defiantly waving goodbye in the slipstream. Adric had seen what Tegan was up to out of the corner of his eye, and been ready for it. Now he gestured to Nyssa. The pair of them ran off after the ambulance at top speed.

With a screech of tyres, Tegan wrenched the wheel round in a tight U-turn, heading the ambulance back towards her two friends. A long way away across the enclosure she could see the main gates, but even as the plan to escape that way formed in her mind the gates began to swing shut and the wail of a warning klaxon fractured the morning air.

Nyssa was nimbler than Adric, and had managed to jump up

on the side of the ambulance, reaching one arm in through the open window and holding on to the outside handle with the other hand. As Tegan swung away in another 180-degree turn, in the rear mirror she saw two of the guards seize hold of Adric. He struggled fiercely, but as more guards arrived he was overpowered.

Tegan reached across the driving seat and helped Nyssa in, steering perilously with one hand as she negotiated her way between a row of huts. 'We'll have to go back for him, I suppose,' she hissed.

Nyssa was already scrambling over the back of the seat into the rear of the ambulance, where the Doctor's stretcher was on the point of slipping out onto the tarmac that raced past below them. 'No, the TARDIS,' Nyssa shouted, grappling with the flapping doors. 'We've got to get the Doctor somewhere safe.'

Adric felt himself being lifted to his feet. 'All right, all right . . . Just let me get my breath back.' There was a crowd around him now, and the strange young boy was never shy when it came to being the centre of attention—even when, as now, his audience was not entirely friendly. Beyond the crowd, some hundred yards away where it had materialised in the shadows at the base of the great radio antenna, he glimpsed the blue telephone box that was the outward guise of the Doctor's time machine, the TARDIS. It meant safety if only he could get to it.

Through the windscreen the two girls could see the TARDIS too. The ambulance was cruising quietly along behind the row of huts, but it seemed inevitable that the big white vehicle would be spotted as soon as they broke cover. The klaxon was still sounding, reminding them that the establishment was swarming with people. There was nothing for it but to take a chance.

Tegan glanced back to make sure the Doctor was secure on the stretcher, crossed her fingers . . . and put her foot down firmly on the accelerator.

The crowd around Adric heard the whine of the accelerating engine and turned to see it hurtling across the enclosure towards the base of the antenna. As the ambulance reached its goal Tegan swung it into a skid so that it ground to a halt with the back doors almost touching the time machine.

'Get the Doctor into the TARDIS,' Tegan snapped. But there

was no need. Nyssa was already scrambling out to open the rear doors.

Adric took advantage of the distraction to renew his struggle with the guards, now that a dozen or so of the staff were headed in the direction of the ambulance. The guards were heavy, but he was good with his feet. Spurred on by the desperate sense that the TARDIS doors might close him out, and leave him marooned forever on this planet of fools and bullies, Adric managed to bring one of them crashing to the ground.

In the distance he could see the girls helping the Doctor out of the ambulance. The two guards had Adric's arm pinned behind him securely now, and he paused for breath, watching with very mixed feelings as the Doctor and the girls disappeared into the safety of the TARDIS. Only a moment later the crowd arrived to batter on the firmly time-locked doors.

Nyssa had reached the door lever just in time. She knew it was the door lever because it was the one control in the TARDIS console room that produced instant, simple and visible results. She surveyed the assembly of dials, buttons and levers in front of her and then looked up at Tegan, who had been struck by the same thought.

'All this technology,' said Tegan, 'and there's nothing we can do with it.'

Nyssa's tone was more practical. 'In any case, we can't take off without Adric. The first thing we must do is get the Doctor somewhere safe . . .' She turned to where they had left him resting, slumped over the console, and caught sight of the small door that led to the TARDIS corridors closing behind a burgundy coat-tail.

'Where's he off to now?' exclaimed Tegan, running after him. Nyssa made a move to follow, but the picture on the big viewer screen caught her eye. It showed Adric being marched across the enclosure by the guards. Was there nothing they could do to help?

Adric had not quite given up trying to explain. 'I suppose you realise the Doctor's just saved us all from the Master. And now he's going to take off, and you'll never have a chance to thank him.' He stopped. No one was listening. The driver had recovered the ambulance, and now it rolled up beside them as

5

they walked towards the main building of the Pharos Project. The driver shouted to the guard through the open window.

'Three of them holed up in that police box thing. Someone's gone off for a key.'

Adric smiled to himself. He knew enough about time translation mechanics to know that the interface was safe from any ordinary Earth device. And that brought him back to the question of how he was going to get in there himself. He hoped the Doctor was well enough to take charge, in which case he could be confident—well, reasonably confident—that some sort of rescue would be organised. Or 'improvised' would be a better expression where the Doctor was concerned. But that last sight of him being dragged like a lifeless bundle into the TARDIS wasn't reassuring. If the Doctor wasn't well enough Adric would have to rely on the girls, and that didn't inspire any confidence at all in the brash young boy.

Adric broke off from his thoughts, suddenly aware that the guards had stopped and were looking upwards, although there was nothing to see in the pale dome of the morning sky but shreds of clouds with a hint of yellow sun behind them. And then the yellowness seemed closer, bringing with it a throbbing sound he had heard before. The colour thickened above them, congealing into a sinister yellow shape as the reverberations grew louder. The Master's TARDIS, still in its Corinthian column configuration, hovered in the air over their heads.

Nyssa saw it too on the viewer screen, and Tegan came running back along the corridor in response to her shout. 'What's the matter?' Nyssa pointed at the screen. The Master's TARDIS was shimmering above the ambulance, and seemed to be sending out some kind of energy that made the people below stagger, draw back and slump to the ground.

Tegan seized the exit lever and the two heavy doors swung open effortlessly. She ran out, calling Adric's name, and Nyssa followed her cautiously out onto the tarmac of the Pharos enclosure.

It was a scene of total confusion. 'Adric!' Tegan shouted, as she began defiantly to approach the Master's TARDIS. 'Adric! Where are you?' As if in answer the Corinthian column swooped up into the air, dispersing the cloud of yellow light and revealing Adric, still on his feet amid the inert bodies.

Tegan and Nyssa ran forward to grab hold of their companion. The boy seemed badly dazed, offering neither assistance nor resistance as the two girls rushed him back towards the TARDIS.

Adric's state of shock persisted even after the double doors had enclosed them all in the safety of the TARDIS. The girls didn't notice at first; there was work to be done. 'I suppose,' said Tegan, 'that we'd better . . . take off . . . or something.' She hesitated in front of the console, gazing at the complexity of buttons and switches.

It was then that the two girls became aware of Adric's intense concentration on the co-ordinate panel. They made way for him as he reached out towards it and began flicking switches and pressing buttons with almost mechanistic precision.

Tegan drew Nyssa aside. 'Are you sure he knows what he's doing?'

'He told me he took off once before,' said Nyssa. 'On Alzarius, his home planet. But that was by mistake, and it almost ended in disaster!'

'Disaster!' echoed Tegan. She turned her head, her eye caught by the time column. It was now alight and already beginning to oscillate. 'I'm sorry I asked, really. Because it looks as if he's done it again.'

The jumble of bodies sprawled across the cold tarmac began to stir into consciousness. The first that were able to raise their heads glimpsed the remarkable sight of the two TARDIS machines, the Master's yellow pillar and the Doctor's blue police box, bleaching out into invisibility. Whether it was the residual effects of the stun ray or some extraordinary trick of acoustics was hard to say, but the unmistakable chuckle of the Master seemed to echo on around the Pharos enclosure long after the throbbing of the time motors had drained away into the morning sky.

2

Towards Zero

The viewer screen showed the planet Earth as a mist-wrapped blue-green sphere receding into the star-filled distance. Nyssa came to stand beside Adric at the console. 'Good take-off,' she said.

But the boy's attention was concentrated on one of the TARDIS control panels, and he didn't even turn his head when Tegan came running back into the room through the small door that led to the corridors. 'The Doctor seems very strange. His mind's wandering. I'm really worried about him.'

'He's bound to be weak,' said Nyssa. 'That's the effect of the regeneration.' She glanced across at Adric, who had told her all she knew about the way Time Lords like the Doctor were able to rebuild themselves. But Adric seemed more concerned with the careful, slow process of setting the co-ordinates.

Tegan shrugged. 'You'd better talk to him, Nyssa. I don't understand any of this scientific stuff. He's gone off after something called the Zero Room.'

Adric looked up abruptly from his labours at the console. 'The Zero Room?' he echoed. 'I'll go.' And without another word he crossed to the small door and went out. Tegan stared after him. 'I like that,' she said, clearly not liking it at all. 'We rescued him, and he never even said thank you.'

Adric had shared many adventures with the Doctor, and knew the TARDIS well. But the internal dimensioning was not like the ordinary architecture he was used to on Alzarius. The great hulk of the Alzarian starliner, in which his people had been forced to winter out the terrible time of Mistfall, was a colony-class ship, constructed of myriad corridors on several levels, but its design was nowhere near as complicated as the configuration of the TARDIS. It wasn't just that they were an enormous maze of twisty corridors, all alike. The Doctor had explained that the TARDIS architecture was 'soft', able to be remoulded at will, as if the rooms and connections between them were made of some kind of logical putty.

The boy was deep inside the ship now, but it was obvious that the Doctor was somewhere nearby. In the last few corridors Adric had been coming across odd bits of debris, clearly emptied out by the Doctor from the copious pockets of his over-coat—perhaps as a way of laying a deliberate trail to be sure of getting back. And now here was the coat itself, lying abandoned on the floor. Further along Adric came across a strand of wool tied to a door handle.

Adric followed the wool. It turned a corner, and then another corner. And there, walking backwards down the corridor, care-fully unravelling his scarf as he went, was the Doctor.

He looked up as Adric approached. The body was stooped, like an old man, but the face under the mop of blond hair was the face of youth, with an open smile and an expression of complete bewilderment in his eyes. It was clear that he didn't recognise Adric.

'Come to help me find the Zero Room, eh?' asked this new Doctor cheerfully, and without waiting for a reply held out a hand, obviously feeling that introductions were necessary. 'Welcome aboard. I'm the Doctor. Or will be, if this regeneration works out.'

'I suppose this is the Mean Free Path Tracker . . . and this panel must be a referential differencer . . .'' Nyssa ran a finger across the console panel, being careful not to alter any of the switch settings. That, unfortunately, was as far as she dared go with her guesses about the console functions. The big disappointment came when she tried to make sense of the co-ordinate patterns Adric had set up. She puzzled over the array of small dials and levers for a long time, but there was no means of knowing where—if anywhere—the TARDIS was headed.

She looked up at the viewer screen. 'Pretty awe-inspiring,'

said Tegan, who had been gazing at the enormous starfield for some time now. 'Infinity.'

'No, not infinity.' Nyssa believed in being accurate. 'There are boundary conditions out there that bring you back to your starting point.'

'That's reassuring. So we'll eventually get back to Earth.'

Nyssa smiled. 'In about a hundred quadrillion years.'

Tegan glanced at her wrist-watch, without appreciating the irony of the connection. Inside the TARDIS ordinary chronology didn't have very much meaning, but she still had a sense that Adric had been gone for a very long time. She left the viewer screen to peep out through the small door that led to the interior.

'I know the TARDIS is huge,' she said over her shoulder to Nyssa. 'But it can't be taking them this long, surely.' The corridor stretching away into the distance showed no signs of life, and there was no sound except the very distant throb of the TARDIS engines. She had once been lost in that maze of white corridors during her involuntary first trip in the TARDIS, and she hated to be reminded of the terrifying experience.

She shut the door and walked back to the console. 'What on earth is a Zero Room, anyway?' she asked Nyssa, who despite being so young seemed to know an awful lot about technology. The Doctor had muttered something about null interfaces, but it was all just gobbledygook to Tegan. She was an outdoor girl.

Nyssa was not like Adric; if she wasn't entirely sure about something technical she said so. 'It sounds as if it might be some sort of neutral environment. An isolated space, cut off from the rest of the universe.'

Tegan laughed. 'If that's all the Doctor needs I could have shown him round Brisbane.'

The Doctor trekked on with no very clear idea of where he was going, although the unravelling of the scarf, which Adric had to help with when it got tangled, left an unequivocal statement of where he had been. With each new twist of the route the hum of the TARDIS engines, though still distant, grew perceptibly louder, but for the past few minutes the sound had been drowned by the Doctor's voice. He was in a voluble mood, excitable and fragile at the same time. Adric couldn't get a word in.

10

'Ordinary spaces show up on the Architectural Configuration Indicators, but any good Zero Room is balanced to zero energy with respect to the world outside its four walls—or however many walls it may have . . . There was a very good polygonal Zero Room under the Junior Senate Block on Gallifrey, with widely acclaimed healing properties. Romana's always telling me I need a holiday.'

Adric broke in. 'Romana's gone, Doctor.' It had been a long time since they had left her to help with Biroc's continuing fight against the slavery of the Tharils.

'Gone! Really! Did she leave a note?'

'We said goodbye to her at the Gateway. Don't you remember?'

The Doctor stopped. 'Oh well, if we did, we did.' But the worried tone in his voice seemed to relate less to the loss of Romana than to the last thin strand of wool he held in his hand. They were so deep into the TARDIS corridors by this time that the scarf, like all good things, had come to an end.

He looped it over a convenient door handle, and said to Adric: 'This should get you back to the Console Room when the time comes.' But as he let go of the handle to move on up the corridor a wave of giddiness hit him, and he staggered momentarily.

'Are you all right, Doctor?'

The Doctor took a moment to steady himself against the wall. 'There are powerful dimensioning forces this deep in the TARDIS. Tend to make you a bit giddy.'

'And the regeneration?'

'Yes, it's taken quite a jolt this time, what with the flood of entropy the Master let loose, and all this dashing about . . . Come along. The sooner we get to this Zero Room place the better . . .' But his general absent-mindedness and the turmoil of the regeneration did not divert the Doctor from the important business of leaving a trail. As the pair of them disappeared round yet another corner, he took off one of his shoes and hooked it onto a door handle.

Nyssa surveyed the console gloomily. 'These mechanisms are too complex. We just can't fly the TARDIS without the

11

Doctor's help.'

We can hardly bank on that, thought Tegan, with another glance at her watch. Anything could have happened to him and Adric. 'Maybe we can just leave it and hope for the best?' she suggested.

'Then the TARDIS will just fly on and on until it crashes into something.' Nyssa made the statement as a scientific fact, and if the idea aroused any emotion in her she didn't show it.

When your whole planet has been wiped out, as Nyssa's Traken had been, personal danger must seem like light relief. But Tegan herself found it hard to be so unconcerned. 'A crash? Is that likely?'

'Inevitable. The star densities in this galaxy vary inversely with the square . . .'

Tegan slammed her fist down on the console and uttered her favourite Antipodean oath. 'Oh, rabbits!' She knew in her heart that Nyssa was probably perfectly right, scientifically speaking, but if those were the facts she felt she had a right to protest against them. If the Laws of Nature were unfair they should be subject to appeal in some higher court.

Nyssa touched Tegan on the shoulder and said quietly: 'Tegan . . . I don't know what's happening to the Doctor—none of us understands it. But I do know that panicking is no use.'

Nyssa touched Tegan on the shoulder and said quietly: 'Tegan . . . I don't know what's happening to the Doctor—none of us understands it. But I do know that panicking is no use.'

Nyssa had already made up her mind. 'There's nothing we can do here. I'm going to try and find them.'

Something in Tegan's tone of voice stopped her at the door. 'No, wait! You don't know those corridors. I got lost in them when I first walked into this ship, and I can tell you, it's a nightmare.'

'Then you'd better stay here,' Nyssa said crisply, opening the door. But she waited for a moment, seeing Tegan biting her lip in indecision.

'I'll come with you,' Tegan said eventually, and ran back to the console to collect her flightbag. She grabbed the shoulder strap and was about to move off when she noticed a small viewer screen that the bag had been hiding. The luminous green lettering on the screen caught her eye. 'Wait a minute!' she called.

Nyssa closed the door and came back to the console. The message was clear and unambiguous. 'TARDIS Relational Information System: Ready for entry.'

'A data bank!' said Nyssa quietly.

Deep in the inner core of the TARDIS the Doctor took off his waistcoat and struggled to rip it in half along the seam. There was still no sign of the Zero Room, but he was rapidly running out of clothing to drop. Now he was left wearing only his shirt, which proved to have a very long tail, like some ancient item of night attire.

As he moved off, some vague memory stirred and made him look back at the ruined half-garment that eked out the trail for one more corridor. 'I left a waistcoat like that on . . .' His mind strained for the place-name . . . and then he found it, and asked the boy: 'Ever been to Alzarius?'

'I was born there, Doctor.'

'Really!' exclaimed the Doctor, genuinely surprised. 'Alzarius . . . well I never . . . Small universe, isn't it.'

Adric's home planet of Alzarius, as the old Doctor had known well, was in fact in a separate negative universe of its own, but now was no moment to quibble. The Doctor had come to a halt at a junction, looking first down one corridor and then down the next, as he tackled the confusing business of deciding between the two.

He turned to Adric. 'I wonder, boy, what you would do if you were me.' A sudden thought seemed to strike him, and he added wrily: 'Or perhaps I should ask—what would I do if I were me?'

From that point on the Doctor's condition deteriorated rapidly. The trail seemed to be forgotten, and a few corridors further on he had to pause to lean against the wall. 'Not far now, Brigadier . . .' he said to Adric, his eyes focused on a non-existent horizon, 'if the Ice Warriors don't get there first . . .'

He shook his head, as if to rectify some faulty component inside his skull, then said more lucidly: 'We've wandered into the wrong corridors . . . We must be close to the Main TARDIS Drive . . .' He turned to the boy, focusing his eyes on Adric with

13

difficulty. 'You go back now. Go back.'

Adric's voice was unnatural, like something heard under-water. 'No, I have to stay with you, Doctor.'

Some of the old fire lit the Doctor's eyes. 'Nonsense, boy, be sensible. Go back . . . Find the trail . . . Don't you understand . . . The regeneration is failing. . . .'

Nyssa was tapping at a keyboard near the small screen of the newly discovered database. Tegan peered over her shoulder. 'Will it tell us how to fly the TARDIS?'

'I'm sure it's in here somewhere, once we find the Index File.'

'And how do we find the Index File?' A silly thought came into Tegan's head. 'Of course, if we had the Index File we could look it up in the Index File under Index File.' The tension was getting to her; she was thinking and talking nonsense.

But Nyssa took it in her stride. Without pausing at her work at the keyboard she said: 'Well done. You've just discovered recursion.' Tegan was surprised to be taken so seriously, but Nyssa went on to explain that recursion was a powerful method used to solve some kinds of mathematical problems. 'It's when procedures fold back on themselves.'

'Oh, I don't understand anything about maths,' Tegan said. She remembered school exams, and how the wretched figures never seemed to stay still on the paper in front of her.

Nyssa laughed when Tegan told her. 'It's not complicated. Here's an example. What's the definition of an ancestor?'

Tegan thought for a minute. 'Well, that's simple. Your ancestor is anybody who is your father, your mother, your father's father, your father's mother, or your mother's mother or . . .' And as she spoke she seemed to see in her mind's eye a long procession of Nyssa's ancestors, a line now completely wiped out as a result of the Master's last evil campaign.

'You call that simple?' Nyssa exclaimed. 'It sounds very complicated. And that only takes you back two generations! But if I say that an ancestor is my mother or my father or any of their ancestors—that's recursion. I call it simple.'

It was certainly simple, Tegan had to agree. 'But the definition just goes round and round. It doesn't tell you what an ancestor is.'

'Doesn't it?' Nyssa asked with a smile. Tegan walked round the console room thinking about it, and at last had to agree that after all it did. 'It's a sort of "if",' she said, delighted to find that there was something mathematical she could understand. If you knew what 'ancestor' meant, you could understand the explanation of the word. So you began by pretending you understood it, and then you . . . sort of . . .

It was a bit mind-boggling when you tried to follow it through logically, like an illustration in a book she remembered seeing somewhere of a picture of a hand drawing a picture of a hand that was drawing the picture of the hand.

'Like the Index File,' she said aloud, as her train of thought brought her back to the starting point of the conversation. 'If you had an Index File you could look it up in the Index File.' Back home in Australia her father always used to say that 'if' was the most powerful word in the language. A wild idea suddenly occurred to her. Knowing the eccentric operation of the TARDIS systems it might just work. 'If!' she exclaimed, running to Nyssa's side. 'I.F. stands for Index File.'

Nyssa and Tegan looked at each other for a moment.

'Well, go on,' said Tegan. 'It's worth a try.'

It was. A moment later the small screen cleared and then rapidly filled up again with luminous green lettering that arranged itself neatly into columns. Tegan, who loved any technology as long as it had something to do with flying, became quite excited at the sight. With her usual air of taking charge she eased Nyssa out of the way and positioned herself in front of the screen. Nyssa suggested she look up 'Destination Setting'.

'Right . . . Destination Setting . . .' Tegan tapped dexterously at the keys. 'Once you get into it, this whole funny system on the TARDIS does start to make a sort of weird sense. . . .' The screen changed again, and Tegan tailed off. The two girls stared in puzzlement at the glowing rectangle. Tegan realised she had spoken too soon. The legend on the screen read:

TARDIS Flight Data. Programmed Journey.
Departure: Earth, Pharos Project.
Destination: Hydrogen Inrush: Event One.

And that didn't make any sense at all.

The Doctor's quest for the Zero Room was going badly. The resting periods had become more and more frequent, and now every turn in the corridor signalled the need to stop for breath. He came to a halt again for the third time in as many minutes and sagged against the wall, but this time he showed no signs of wanting to press on.

Adric watched him without moving. The ordeal seemed to be affecting the boy too, for there was a strangely unfocused look in his eye, and an odd rigidity of his body. Several moments passed, with the Doctor struggling inwardly with this unfamiliar weakness, and Adric, a cold unmoving observer.

Then the boy began backing away down the corridor. Sensing his absence the Doctor raised his head and called after him: 'Adric!' Somewhat unsteadily the Doctor detached himself from the wall. 'Adric? Not that way. Adric . . .!' He broke off and thought for a moment. Adric—yes, that was the boy's name. Odd that he hadn't remembered it before.

And odder still, come to think of it, that he remembered it now, with the boy moving away from him, as if some sort of inverse square law were at work. And if indeed it was Adric's sudden absence that had revived the Doctor's memory, perhaps the same phenomenon was beginning to revive his strength, for now he was finding it easier to breathe.

He stretched, straightened up, and set off after the boy.

Tegan had forgotten her qualms about exploring the corridors as soon as they had come across the trail of discarded clothing. 'Shouldn't be too hard to find him now,' she called out to Nyssa. When they reached the beginning of the scarf she pointed out the thread of wool to Nyssa. 'The poor old Doctor's coming unravelled in more ways than one. Look, I'm going to be all right with this on my own. Hadn't you'd better go back to the console room?'

Nyssa shook her head. 'I've no idea where we're going, but according to the data bank we're on some kind of programmed flight. We won't crash.' Tegan would have found this reassuring, if, in the interest of strict scientific accuracy, Nyssa hadn't felt constrained to add: 'At least, I don't think so.'

It was so long since the Doctor had last ventured this deep into the TARDIS that he had forgotten all about this area, where the dusty rooms held many remnants of old enthusiasms. One sharp reminder of earlier and more leisurely days was waiting for him in the corridor as he turned a corner—a hatstand, very like the one in the console room, bore a crop of hats of various kinds, and a white umpire's coat. At its base lay a pair of green Wellington boots, giving it an almost human appearance.

But it was the full-length mirror attached to the wall beside the hatstand that first arrested the Doctor's attention. All thoughts of pursuit of the boy (which had seemed so urgent for some reason that had already slipped his mind) were chased out of his head when he caught sight of his reflection.

For reasons that had nothing to do with personal vanity, this glimpse of a slim, fair-haired young man in a long white shirt that came down almost to his ankles brought him to an abrupt halt. He stepped closer to the glass, contemplating his new face without much enthusiasm.

'The trouble with regeneration . . .' the Doctor confided to the equally dazed figure on the other side of the silvered surface, 'is that you never quite know what you're going to get.' He was on the point of moving off when he noticed a black handle protruding from one of the Wellington boots. He drew it out, and the weight of the willow in his hand brought back sunlit memories that smelled of new-mown grass.

He held the cricket bat up to his eye and looked along it approvingly. A thorough rub-down with linseed oil and it would be as good as ever. He had an idea that there was a bottle in the locker in the old pavilion. He pushed open the door near the hatstand, and a deep nostalgia came over him at the sight of the white sweaters on a line of brass hooks, the single dusty cricket pad, the cricket ball on the changing-room bench.

Nyssa looked up from inspecting the Doctor's torn waistcoat. 'This part of the TARDIS can't have been used for centuries.'

Tegan had been scouting ahead. 'That looks like the end of the trail,' she said, walking back down the corridor. 'But the corridors just seem to go on and on.'

Pretending not to notice the uneasiness in her friend's voice,

17

Nyssa opened a door to peep into another room that offered a glimpse of hibernating humps of furniture under dustcovers. She was not to know that a second door led out from the other side of that room into a similar corridor, where at that very moment, Adric was walking briskly, moving with an oddly mechanical motion, his eyes unnaturally wide, his expression blank. His pace quickened, as if forces beyond his own will were driving him on, until the walk had become a run.

Nyssa shut the door and paused to listen. But what sounded like the echo of hurrying footsteps from some nearby corridor may only have been a resonance in the conduits behind the wall panels.

'On and on,' Tegan repeated, as they moved off again. 'And deeper and deeper.'

'Yes, I get that feeling too—that we're going downwards,' said Nyssa. 'Although of course there's no scientific basis for it.'

With no trail to follow, the chances of finding the Doctor and Adric were getting slimmer by the minute. Not for the first time it seemed to Tegan that the TARDIS, a friendly enough vehicle in the regular way of things, could be a very dangerous place without the Doctor at your elbow.

With all this to think of, it was just as well that neither of the two friends knew anything of the imminent danger that threatened from outside.

The pursuing ship was close enough to monitor the interior activity in the TARDIS. The viewer screen, cutting a great window of light in the murky black walls of the control room, scanned the indented roundels that were the curious Palladian feature of the TARDIS corridors. But the boy was moving fast, and even the poly-directrix lenses, enhancements that among many others gave this vehicle an enormous technical advantage over the Doctor's early Type 40, did not succeed completely in holding the urgently running image firmly focused.

A black-gloved hand reached out to make a delicate adjustment. Dynanometer needles kicked on the instrument panel, pulling Adric's face into the screen until it filled the frame with its wide-open eyes and strangely hard-set mouth.

The Master leaned back, permitting himself a thin chuckle that floated away into a whisper. 'Oh, no, you can't escape.

You're mine, Adric, mine—until we have completed our final task.'

3

Destination: Event One

The Doctor stepped back into the corridor with the cricket bat that now gleamed with linseed oil and smelled reassuringly of fresh putty and newly glazed windows. The cricket trousers he had adopted could perhaps have done with a pressing, but they were clean, and in combination with the V-neck sweater imbued him with a general effect of whiteness that was casually elegant.

He slipped the bat back into the green Wellington boot, and was drawn once more by his image in the mirror. Among his old sporting gear he had found a cream-coloured garment that was too summery to be a morning coat but too long to be a sports jacket. He tried it on now, and consulted the mirror for its opinion. The coat was not altogether right for him, but then he had to admit he wasn't altogether right for the coat either. He was on the point of arriving at the decision that they would give each other a try, at least for the moment, when a rumbling, running sound made him stop to listen.

The noise halted abruptly, punctuated by the banging of a door slammed shut, which echoed eerily down great distances of corridor. The Doctor caught his breath, tolled back instantly from his leather-and-willow dreams of village greens. 'That's it! That's the door!' he exclaimed, and moved off quickly in the direction of the sound.

He hadn't gone far, at least by the standards of the TARDIS corridor system, when he stumbled on Nyssa and Tegan. Worn out by the uncountable rooms they had looked into by now, the two girls had heard the door-slam too and were running towards it from the opposite direction. Meeting them almost forcibly at a junction, the Doctor reeled back unsteadily, and with no social preliminaries shouted: 'The Zero Room door. I heard it slam.'

'Doctor! Thank Heavens! Are you all right?'

The Doctor focused on Tegan. 'Fit as a fiddle, Vicky. But there's something very peculiar going on in the TARDIS. The Zero Room—have you seen it anywhere about?'

Tegan pointed along the corridor. 'The noise came from this way.'

The Doctor seemed content to follow them, as though he were no longer certain of his own judgement. But it was hard to be sure of anything, this deep in the TARDIS, where the corridors were twistier than ever. But one feature attracted the Doctor's attention, and he stopped to examine the TARDIS wall.

'Hello,' said the Doctor, greeting the thin uneven red line with a courtesy he had denied the girls, 'a carmine seepage.'

Tegan held up her lipstick dispenser. 'Matter of fact, Doctor, that's me.' They had been round that way already, and as an aid to navigation Tegan had had the idea of marking the walls.

The Doctor took the small gold cylinder from her and held it up for inspection. 'That's a relief. I thought the TARDIS auto-systems were playing up again. Dreadful . . . always going wrong. It's time we went to Logopolis to get it sorted out once and for all.'

Tegan was about to point out that they had already been to Logopolis, when Nyssa, who had been continuing her methodical search for the room called back along the corridor: 'Doctor . . . What does the Zero Room look like?'

The Doctor answered distractedly—he was balancing the lipstick dispenser on a small shelf that ran along the corridor—'Zero Room? Oh, well . . . it's very big. Empty. Grey . . .'

Nyssa stood in a doorway, looking into a room that exactly fitted that description.

Tegan had never seen anything like it in her life before, although later, when she thought about that moment of entering through the big double doors, she realised that it wasn't particularly the look of the Zero Room that so impressed her. Certainly the place was big—vast, in fact, in its pinkish-grey emptiness, bathed somehow in a warm light reminiscent of a late-summer afternoon. The walls were indented with the familiar TARDIS roundels that you saw everywhere else on the ship—but here they were huge, forming high curved shelves big enough to climb onto.

The really remarkable thing was the sensation of utter peace that descended on the three of them the moment they were inside. The Doctor came to his senses quite suddenly.

'Thank you,' he said, turning to Tegan with a very polite if slightly crumpled smile that matched the cricketing outfit perfectly. 'You must be Tegan.' He had remembered her name! It was like having the old Doctor with them again. He gestured to where the other girl was standing, craning up at the high ceiling, hypnotised by the deep silence. 'It'll work even better if you shut the doors, Nyssa.'

Nyssa reached out into the corridor and pulled on the ornate bronze handles. As the doors closed, the silence, if such a thing were possible, seemed to become deeper still. A cool, slightly sweet odour pervaded the air, which took Tegan a moment to identify. 'Roses?' she said in a whisper.

The Doctor nodded. 'Yes, I've never understood why. Quite peaceful, isn't it.'

Nyssa had known peace something like this before. It reminded her of her home planet before the devastating arrival of the Master. 'Will you have to stay in here for long, Doctor?' she asked.

'Just until my dendrites heal again. The nervous system's a very delicate network of logic junctions . . .'

'The synapses, yes,' Nyssa nodded seriously.

The Doctor smiled. It had slipped his memory that bio-electronics was her strong point. 'Yes, well, my tussle with the Master came at exactly the wrong moment. When the synapses are weak they're like radio receivers, picking up all sorts of jumbled signals.'

Tegan was anxious not to be left out of this technical conversation. 'I get it—the Zero Room cuts out all the interference.'

'Completely. Even the gravity's only local.' The Doctor jumped lightly up and down on his toes by way of demonstration, but the exercise made him yawn. 'Goodness me, I'm tired.'

The girls looked round the vast baroque emptiness, but there was no bed to be seen, not even an armchair. The Doctor seemed to read their thoughts. 'I don't need a bed. Not in the Zero Room.' And very slowly he began to lean back on his heels, until he reached an impossible angle, whereupon he lifted his feet and rose until he was hovering about four feet off the floor.

He smiled at the astonished expressions on the faces of his two friends. 'One of the great advantages of stark simplicity.'

'Strewth!' exclaimed Tegan. 'Can anybody do that?'

The Doctor gracefully rotated into a completely horizontal position. 'You don't do it. It . . . sort of . . . comes upon you.' He yawned again. 'Like sleep. Very like . . . sleep.'

He closed his eyes, and with a slight gesture of one hand which they understood immediately, gathered the two girls towards him. Now his voice seemed to come from very far away. 'We only just reached the Zero Room in time. This regeneration is going to be difficult, and I shall need you all, every one of you. You, Tegan, have it in you to be a fine Co-ordinator, keeping us all together during the Healing Time. Nyssa of course, has the technical skills and understanding. The information you will need is all there in the TARDIS data bank—I'm sure you'll find your way to it.'

'We already have, Doctor,' Tegan told him eagerly.

The Doctor's voice was receding further and further into the distance. 'Good, good, of course you have . . . And Adric, with his badge for Mathematical Excellence . . . Adric is the navigator. He knows the way, and he knows me, my old self. Adric, you must help me heal the disconnection.' The voice was faint now, and they had to strain to listen to the last words. 'Your role is crucial . . .'

And then the voice was gone. The Doctor was utterly still, suspended in his death-like trance.

Adric! Nyssa and Tegan exchanged a glance. But if the Doctor didn't know where the boy was—then who did? Should they wake him with the news that they had lost their Navigator? Together they stood beside the Doctor for a long time, and it struck Tegan how perfectly natural, in the context of the Zero Room, the otherwise extraordinary phenomenon of his floating on air seemed to be. Everything in the Zero Room seemed, in its own way, to float—even time itself. But the next thing that happened came with heart-stopping suddenness.

Nyssa was the first to see it. She had raised her head to survey the huge domed ceiling, and now she gasped and pointed towards one of the nearby walls. Tegan turned to look, and her hand rushed to her mouth to suppress a scream. Up on one of the roundels, spread-eagled in the centre of the circle like a fly struggling in an invisible web, was their friend Adric.

Nyssa called out his name, running towards the desperate figure of the boy, who seemed to be fighting for breath and trying to communicate with them.

'Adric . . . What are you doing?' Tegan almost screamed, but there was no echo in the Zero Room, and the sound died away immediately.

The boy managed to force out a few choked syllables. 'A trap . . . He set a trap . . . The Master . . .'

Nyssa cupped a hand to her ear to catch the words. 'The Master! Where?'

'Me! I'm the trap. I locked the co-ordinates . . . Event One . . .'

Tegan had been looking round for something she could use to climb up to him. 'Just you hold on. I'm coming to help you,' she shouted with a confidence she did not feel, for the vast room remained resolutely empty.

Adric tried to shake his head, but the wall was sucking at his hair. He seemed to be warning the girls to stay back. 'This isn't me! It isn't me! A projection . . . Block Transfer. Tegan—the co-ordinates.' And even before they had grasped the meaning of his words, the image of Adric began to break up, like a television set in need of repair, shattering the peace of the Zero Room with the hiss of static.

And then the image was gone, leaving the girls to stare up in horror at the empty roundel where their friend had seemed to be.

The Master chuckled, looking up at the boy from the console that had been controlling the projection. Adric hung, quite lifeless now, suspended in the electronic web of glittering little wires that criss-crossed through his flesh. Only his wide-open eyes betrayed his will to live and to escape.

Master was conscious of this problem, but then new technologies always had their development difficulties. 'So, these simulated projections are real enough to have a will of their own. Almost.'

Adric stared insolently back. 'Can't reach me in the Zero Room . . .'

Master's smile was like a sliver of ice. 'Is that what you thought? But my dear young man, it is your own computational powers that make the Block Transfer possible. If escape were that easy, Adric, we could all be free of this nasty world.' And with that, the Master worked a lever on the console. Breath sighed out of the boy's body, and his angry eyes closed. 'We must save your energies. There is so much yet to be done.'

'We can't tell him now. He's in a dangerously unstable state.' Nyssa glanced back at the Doctor, who was still suspended peacefully in his levitational trance. Clearly Adric had been trying to warn them of something, but they were going to have to work out what it was without the Doctor's help. She ran over in her mind the few words Adric had been able to utter. 'The co-ordinates. And something about a trap,' she said aloud, but Tegan was as baffled as she was.

And then a rather unpleasant thought struck her. There was no point in alarming Tegan with it, if, as she hoped, there was nothing in the idea, but it certainly needed investigating. She called over her shoulder to Tegan: 'You stay here and keep an eye on the Doctor.'

Tegan ran into the corridor after her. 'Where are you going?'

'Console room. You look after the Doctor.' And before Tegan had time to argue the girl had disappeared around a bend in the corridor.

Tegan pulled the double doors shut, and the monumental stillness of the Zero Room closed around her again. She couldn't help raising her eyes to the roundel where Adric had appeared. She found it hard to believe that it was just a projected image, but Nyssa knew about these things, and had assured her it was possible. But if that wasn't really Adric, where was he? If only there were something she could do to help him.

She heard a soft bump behind her, and looked back to find that the Doctor had come to rest on the floor. He opened his eyes and asked, in an ordinary tone of voice: 'What's the matter?'

'Sorry,' said Tegan. 'I didn't mean to wake you.'

The Doctor sat up, brushing a few of the newer creases from his cream-coloured coat. 'Excuse a note of carping criticism, but there seems to be something distinctly wrong. I can feel it.'

Tegan struggled with herself. It was so tempting to tell the Doctor everything, but she remembered Nyssa's warning.

Nyssa loosened her collar. The corridors were warm after the Zero Room, and as she followed the lipstick trail that Tegan had been sensible enough to leave, they seemed to get warmer and warmer. Her first conjecture was that this must be some sort of psychological effect, like the sense of descending that had accompanied them on the way towards the Zero Room, a phenomenon now matched by the distinct feeling that she was going upwards. But then she noticed that in places the lipstick trail was beginning to drip down the wall.

She stopped to touch it, and the stain came off on her finger like liquid. Perhaps it was her imagination, but the wall at this point seemed noticeably warmer than usual.

The important business was getting back to the console room to check the flight information and see if there was any truth in the unpleasant thought that had occurred to her, so she pushed the question of the walls and their unnatural warmth to the back of her mind. But when she arrived at the junction where the Doctor had put down the lipstick dispenser the sight of it standing on the corridor shelf with red liquid oozing out of its base reminded her again of the heat problem.

She picked it up, and some of the contents spilled onto the floor. Gingerly she put her hands on various parts of the corridor walls. There was no doubt about it—the ambient heat level was up, and rising.

She began to walk briskly now, driven by the realisation that there might well be a connection between this new phenomenon and her uneasy speculations about the possible fate of the TARDIS. And at that moment, as if the TARDIS systems had made the same connection, a doleful tolling sound came rolling towards her down the corridors.

She recognised the cloister bell, the warning mechanism that signalled only the direst emergencies.

Inside the Zero Room, faintly, the Doctor and Tegan heard it too. The Doctor held his finger to his lips, and for a long time stood frozen in that gesture of silence, listening to the omen as if its nuances carried some special message for him.

'We're in danger, aren't we?' said Tegan eventually.

'Worse than that. The TARDIS is in danger. Who's in the console room?'

'Nyssa . . .' Tegan said quickly, hoping that the inevitable question wouldn't follow. But it did.

'And Adric?'

The thought of having to lie to the Doctor made Tegan very uncomfortable. 'Adric? He's . . .'

'Well, is he or isn't he?' asked the Doctor, showing signs of irritation.

Tegan took a deep breath. It was no good—she would have to tell him. But impelled by growing impatience, the Doctor was already heading for the Zero Room door. Tegan ran to stop him. 'No! You're not to go out there, Doctor!'

Before she could get to him the Doctor had pushed open the big double doors. It was just as well she reached him when she did, because an invisible concrete wall seemed to be waiting for him in the corridor, and he walked straight into it. His knees buckled and he reeled back. Tegan managed to catch him, and dragged him into the Zero Room again as fast as she could.

The Doctor recovered quickly, although his breathing was still fast. 'Adric,' he said, 'you mentioned something about Adric.'

'Adric isn't . . .'

'Adric isn't what? Tell me . . .'

'Adric isn't relevant,' said Tegan, her mind made up. 'Look, Doctor, you're obviously going to be perfectly OK as long as you stay here.' And before he could interrupt, she was already at the door. 'I'm going to the console room to sort this all out. After all, I am the Co-ordinator.'

The lipstick trail had led to the trail of the Doctor's clothes, and by following that Nyssa found her way back to the console room relatively easily, although with the rising temperature thin fingers of smoke had begun to trickle up between the floor plates. She closed the door, muting the continuous moan of the cloister bell, and ran over to the console, where a message was flashing on the small screen.

'Approaching Hydrogen Inrush, Event One,' it said. And then as she read it a new sentence appeared, in big capital letters: ENVIRONMENT BEYOND ENGINEERING TOLERANCES. Nyssa stared at the message. Its meaning was clear enough, but she had no idea what she was supposed to do about it.

If the heat and the tolerance warning were linked with this mysterious Event One, then it seemed that the sensible thing would be to find out what the Hydrogen Inrush actually was. She began a patient search of the data base. Like the walls, the keyboard was now hot to the touch, and she worked fast, hoping she would be able to track down the information before the system collapsed.

At first reading the entry under 'Hydrogen' didn't tell her anything that she didn't know already. '. . . abundant element, highly explosive in the presence of oxygen . . . Found throughout the universe in its dioxide form as ice, water or water vapour . . .'

But when she came to read it again her attention was riveted by one phrase. 'Hydrogen is the basic constituent out of which the galaxy was first made . . .' The dreadful suspicion that had seized her in the Zero Room seemed to be confirmed.

Tegan arrived at that moment, very hot and distraught. 'Typical TARDIS, choosing a time like this for the air-conditioning to collapse.'

If only that were the trouble,' said Nyssa. 'It's not the inside of the TARDIS we have to worry about.'

'What else could it be?'

Nyssa led her over to the viewer screen. 'You'd better have a look at this.' Puzzled, Tegan duly read the entry on 'Hydrogen', thinking that Nyssa was being rather schoolmarmish about all this, and wondering why she couldn't just tell her whatever it was she had discovered. But when at last she looked up from the small screen she knew why Nyssa was being so careful about breaking the news to her. You needed some technical understanding to realise the terrible thing that was happening.

The two friends looked at each other, and Tegan had the courage to speak first. 'This is a time machine . . . And the Master's turned it into a trap.'

So that was the terrible thing that Adric, or rather the image of him controlled by the Master, had done to the TARDIS co-ordinates. They were racing towards the First Event, the creation of the galaxy out of a huge inrush of hydrogen.

Nyssa nodded. 'We're heading straight into an explosion.'

'Explosion?' Tegan queried, as if a quibble could stave off the reality of the event. 'How can an inrush be an explosion.'

'We'll be entering it backwards in time,' Nyssa answered coolly. 'The biggest explosion in history.' And at that moment the TARDIS gave a sudden lurch, throwing the two girls against the walls, which were by this time very hot to the touch.

In the Zero Room the persistent tolling of the cloister bell had been nagging at the Doctor like an aching tooth. Something was very badly wrong, and he had to find out what it was and put it right. Cautiously this time he began to nudge open one of the big double doors, leaning back against the other as it swung gently open.

When the first lurch came it sent the Doctor spinning out into the corridor. And then when the TARDIS began to shake he reached out for a handhold, the handle of a nearby door. It was not the most sensible thing to do, but by this time the Doctor was hardly in a sensible mood. The door swung open, connecting with his head, and he slid down it to the ground, unconscious.

Nyssa and Tegan had barely had time to recover and stagger back towards the console when the second lurch sent them flying again. Tegan grabbed for a handhold, which happened to be a console control. Random handling of the instrument panel was a dangerous business, and she was lucky that all that happened was that the door of the viewer screen slid open. But when she looked up and saw what the screen depicted she gasped.

The face of their hated enemy, the Master, grinned down at them and they saw a black-gloved hand waving in a gesture of farewell. As the image retreated, flashing lights revealed something of the interior of his vehicle. The black walls, the gleaming instrument panel . . . and behind them, Adric, caught in the glittering web of steel mesh.

The Master spun away into the distant starfield leaving the Doctor's TARDIS to its fateful destination. The two girls stared in horror at the empty screen.

4

Russian Roulette

Long after the Master's vehicle had spun away into the distant starfield, Nyssa went on looking at the viewer screen, seeming to see there the hated face of the man who had killed her father and destroyed her whole planet. Tegan stood beside her, anxious to do something, although it was hard to know what.

'There's only one thing we can do,' Nyssa said after what seemed like a long silence. She slammed her hand on the lever that activated the viewer screen, and the cover slid shut again.

'And then what?' asked Tegan.

Nyssa's response came coolly. 'That's all.'

'All! Hogwash!' Tegan raised her voice indignantly. 'We've found the data bank—we can learn to fly the machine.' The TARDIS seemed to have taken note of her bravura, because at that moment it gave another enormous lurch.

Deep in the interior of the eccentric Gallifreyan craft the same lurch caused a chrome and glass medical trolley to waddle out through a door marked 'Surgery', and sent it rattling off down the corridor towards the point where the Doctor lay hunched up on the ground. By one of those useful coincidences that so often spiced the Doctor's life, the trolley carried on its top shelf a large tin box bulging with medical supplies. But as mischance would have it (and the Doctor always had his fair share of that as well) he was too profoundly unconscious to take advantage of the fact, even when the trolley thudded gently into his shoulder.

The tin box tottered precariously above the Doctor's head, while the TARDIS veered giddyingly in space, speeding towards its doom. And then the Doctor chose to stir, which again was unfortunate, because as he tried to prop himself up he jogged the trolley. The dislodged box landed on his head sharp corner downwards and scattered its contents all over the floor.

The sudden well-defined pain dragged him back to consciousness. He reached for a nearby roll of cotton wool and pulled off a wad to dab on his head. The trolley, having delivered its load of emergency medical supplies, succumbed to further motion of the TARDIS and went rolling off along the corridor.

The Doctor tried hard to pull himself together; with all these bottles and pills at his feet there was no excuse to prolong the malingering. He certainly did not feel very fit, but he knew from centuries of experience that one's own feelings are not necessarily the best guide to the real state of things. He fumbled among the packets of pills and small bottles of liquid, raising each in turn to his eyes to study it carefully and see if it had a contribution to make.

And then the TARDIS began to shake again, as if there were a race of demons in the superstructure. In the distance the cloister bell tolled on.

From the safety and comfort of his own travelling machine the Master watched on his viewer screen the violent shaking of his rival's vehicle as all the stars of the starfield began to close in around it. Behind him the boy hung in the cruel mesh of the electronic web, able only to stare in horror at the fate of his friends and the ship that had carried him on so many adventures.

He heard the familiar chuckle he had come to dread, and looked down to meet a pair of dark eyes that seemed to pierce his skull and read his mind. 'You must control these dangerous emotions, Adric. They only cause you pain.'

The Master turned back to the viewer screen and adjusted a small knob on the control panel. 'Besides which, your emotions interfere with reception.' Certainly something was causing small white streaks on the picture. 'Let us go in closer.' On the screen the image of the TARDIS swelled, and the tiny wires that riddled Adric's flesh hummed faintly with the surge of energy they sucked from the boy.

The Master studied the screen, but the quality of the image dissatisfied him. He closed a switch on the console and turned back to the Alzarian. 'You have something to say?' the mocking voice enquired. 'Well?'

'I'll fight you . . .' Adric managed through the pain. 'I won't help you harm the Doctor.'

'Such touching loyalty.' Condescension purred in the Master's voice. 'But no match for my voltages.' He adjusted a lever and the pain that surged through Adric's body cleared the picture on the screen. A second lever dissolved the screen into a blue mist as the poly-directrix lenses penetrated the outer plasmic wall of the TARDIS.

'Closer, Adric,' came the insidious, insisting voice. 'I want to see them.' The Master moved the lever again, the glitter of victory in his eyes.

The Doctor had inspected all the small bottles, but witch hazel, friar's balsam, distilled glycerine, peppermint essence and oil of bergamot, though each excellent in its way, did not, he felt, quite meet the present case. He was left with the last of them, a small green container with a label that uncompromisingly announced itself as: 'The Solution'. The Doctor shook his head. 'Ah, my little friend . . . if only you were.'

At that moment the oceanic heaving of the TARDIS threw up more flotsam, for down the corridor a splendid visitation came rolling towards him: a motorised wheelchair. 'Ah, Transport of Delight!' cried the Doctor, stretching out a hand as it cruised within his reach.

The smoke was growing denser in the TARDIS console room, and it was now very nearly too hot to breathe. Tegan knew the risks of meddling with the TARDIS controls—even the Doctor, who understood the eccentricities of the old Type 40 better than anybody, sometimes came unstuck. But having brushed aside Nyssa's cautious reservations, she was determined to get a response from at least one of these myriad buttons and levers. After all, she had flown her father's Cessna back in Australia, and that had seemed horrendously complicated before you got used to it. And the worst that could happen as a result couldn't be anything near as dangerous as the Hydrogen Inrush to which the TARDIS was so determinedly heading.

But in fact nothing at all happened, even when she and Nyssa had walked round the console twice trying every switch and lever.

Nyssa had already explained that there wasn't much point to all this frenzied activity. Even if they managed to adjust the trim of the TARDIS they still couldn't change course. They were already caught in the field of Event One, which was pulling them faster and faster towards inevitable destruction. It is all very well being in at the beginning of things, but not when you are hurtling backwards into it at the speed of light.

Tegan was slow to grasp the physics of the situation. 'This force—it's a sort of gravity?'

'The Time Force. It's like gravity, but many orders of magnitude more powerful.'

Tegan took this as agreement with her idea, and developed it. 'People escape from gravity all the time. All we need is some kind of rocket thrust.' She caught Nyssa's eye. 'All right, enormous thrust . . . There must be some way the TARDIS can do that.'

'We can't even develop thrust,' Nyssa explained. 'The temperature's defeating the automatic controls . . .'

Tegan looked round the oppressive, smoke-filled console room in despair, and silently appealed to the spirit of the TARDIS, or whatever you called the obstinate thing that drove it. Of the various responses she could reasonably—or unreasonably—have expected, the one that came was the most surprising of all. The small door that led to the corridors chose that moment to open, ushering in a crumpled cream-clad figure riding in an electric wheelchair.

'Doctor!' the two girls gasped together. And Nyssa added immediately: 'You must go back!'

The Doctor replied with a lively shake of the head. 'Smoke . . . heat . . . noise . . . Adrenalin! Neuro-peptides . . .' He tapped the side of his skull. 'The brain's working.'

'Neuro-peptides?' asked Tegan. 'What's he on about now?'

Nyssa knelt in front of the Doctor, looking at him closely. 'The excitement's changing his biochemistry. It's only temporary, what they call a remission, but perhaps he can help us.'

Certainly the Doctor had a high flush in his otherwise pale cheeks, but that might just have been the temperature, for the console room was like a Turkish bath in which someone was trying to light a bonfire. 'You're right,' said Tegan. 'Better take him back straight away. It's not safe.'

But Nyssa's scientific mind had by now had time to work on the possibilities and probabilities, and she shook her head. 'The Doctor's our only chance . . . unless we can find some way of getting the temperature down.'

The note of urgency in her voice seemed to strike a chord in the Doctor, for he sat upright, suddenly completely alert. 'Manual over-ride. Nyssa . . . I'll have to explain how to vent the thermo-buffer . . .' A long arm stretched out to draw her closer to him. 'Listen carefully. My concentration may go again any minute . . .'

The poly-directrix lenses were focused sharply now, and although there was no means of picking up sound vibrations across so many parsecs of empty space, the Master fancied he could hear the dialogue of despair as the two girls huddled around the Doctor.

From behind him, up on the web, the boy's voice came as a faint commentary on the silent picture: 'Doctor!'

The Master smiled thinly. 'I sympathise. This is all too easy.' On the screen both girls were kneeling in front of the wheelchair now, paying attention to some fruitless final observations the Doctor saw fit to make. The obstinacy of the man in the face of assured total defeat stirred the Master's admiration. 'A great pity. These facile victories only leave me hungry for more conquests.'

The TARDIS had ceased to fight the pull of the Time Force. Nyssa knew this meant that technically they had passed the point of no return, and were headed smoothly on course to destruction. But she had to put the thought from her mind, and bury it under the urgent work of the moment. She concentrated on repeating the instructions the Doctor had given her: a thermal gradient of minus 800 . . . reverse Kelvin effect . . . transition temperatures for the outer-shell coolants. She received his approval, and crossed quickly to the door that led to the corridors.

The chimes of the cloister bell came so regularly now that she hardly heard them, but she needed no reminder of the emergency, for the smoke stung her eyes until she could hardly see for tears. It smelled acrid, as if important components were beginning to burn behind the walls, but she kept to the route, moving quickly but not running. At the third junction she turned right, and then right again.

The roundel looked like all the rest, and had it not been for the Doctor's careful instructions she could have searched the corridors forever without finding it. The circular panel came out of the wall quite easily as she turned it, and somehow managed to remain illuminated even when she put it down on the floor.

Behind the panel, just as the Doctor had said, was a white space, with a small silver pointer in the centre. The moment she reached in to touch it the dreadful clamour of the cloister bell stopped dead, and the silence fell on her ears like a sea of snow-drifts.

In the console room the Doctor heard it too, and stopped in the middle of rattling off rapid instructions to Tegan. 'Good,' he said, sniffing the air, as though he could smell the silence through the wreaths of smoke, 'The whole system is on manual now. This is where it gets dangerous . . .'

Tegan had written, in not very accurate Pitman's shorthand, '. . . and you'll always find it simpler if you go into hover mode first . . .' Her pencil paused over the notepad. 'You mean it's been perfectly safe up to now!'

The Doctor chose to ignore the joke. 'The temperature will start coming down fairly quickly. That's good for you and the TARDIS, but bad for me. Without the stimulus my neuro-peptide level will fall to normal.'

'Don't worry, Doc. We'll get you straight back to the Zero Room.'

'Good. Now, as soon as full console functions are restored you"! be able to reprogram the Architectural Configuration . . .' He levered himself stiffly up out of the wheelchair. 'This bit's very tricky. I'd better show you.'

They leant over the console together and the Doctor ran very quickly through the rudiments of dimensioning theory, just enough to give some meaning to the string of tasks she would have to perform. Tegan nodded and said 'Uh-huh' even when she didn't quite understand, because she thought that theory was all very well, but she wanted to get on to the doing part of it.

She had to stop the Doctor's flow for one important question though. 'What I don't quite see is, how will it help to change the TARDIS rooms around?'

'The Architectural Configuration System does more than that. We can actually delete rooms.'

Tegan opened her eyes in surprise. 'Delete them! You mean, just . . . zap??'

'Exactly . . . zap. Enough zap, and you'll have your thrust.' He directed her direction to a set of switches in a little niche by themselves on the console. 'Now follow this carefully.'

'You bet your life, Doc.'

The Master smiled up at Adric, gesturing towards the screen. 'Perhaps this little demonstration is giving you some glimpse of my real power.'

The boy stared back defiantly. Though weak and unable to move, his face gave fluent expression to his feelings. 'Power you're getting from me . . . My computations.'

Without any visible cue from the Master, the black wall suddenly unfolded to reveal something like a small escalating staircase, which rolled forward automatically. The Master stepped onto the device, and to the accompaniment of a faint whirring sound was carried upwards until he could peer closely into Adric's face.

'Your computations?' purred the Master. 'In part, certainly. Even as an enemy you're useful. But how much more useful as an ally . . .' He looked into Adric's eyes, giving the invitation time to sink in.

Tegan read her notes again to make quite sure she understood what the Doctor had told her. 'So we're converting the mass of the deleted TARDIS rooms into momentum. And that should give us the thrust we need to get out of this Inrush thing.' She understood most of it, except what 'momentum' was.

'Mass in motion. Thrust, if you like. Time enough for lessons later.'

'But it means burning up part of the TARDIS?' The Doctor seemed to take it lightly, but Tegan found the idea very disturbing.

'Don't worry, it works,' said the Doctor, misunderstanding what was troubling her. 'We had to do that once with Adric to get away from . . .' And then he asked the question she had been dreading. 'By the way, where is Adric?'

Tegan blushed. 'He's . . . Adric's . . .'

Doctor was impatient for an answer. 'Well, where?—We need him.'

Nyssa turned the pointer and the colour of the space behind the roundel slowly changed, going down through the colours of the rainbow until it became a deep cerulean blue. By the time she had put back the panel the smoke was already beginning to dissipate in the corridors, and it had become noticeably cooler.

She arrived back in the console room just in time to hear the Doctor asking about Adric's whereabouts, and her reappearance at that moment gave Tegan a split second to think.

'It's cooler out there in the corridors already, that's something,' Nyssa announced, by way of a distraction. But deceiving the Doctor made her feel uncomfortable, and in response to Tegan's raised eyebrows telegraphing for help across the room she took a deep breath and stepped forward. 'We have to talk to you about Adric, Doctor. You see . . .'

Tegan began her explanation at the same time. 'We thought Adric was in the Zero Room, but . . .'

As it happened, the Doctor wasn't listening to either of them. He had noticed the screen, where the starfield was getting visibly denser by the minute. 'Tell me later,' he said, much to their relief. 'There's not much time. Once the starfield approaches critical mass we'll be shut into the Inrush. Where were we?' He took the notebook from Tegan's hand, but the wriggling pencil-marks told him nothing, although he had learnt shorthand once, a long time ago. Then he caught sight of the rubber on the end of her pencil. 'Ah yes, deleting rooms.' He was beginning to look a little unsteady on his feet. He groped for the wheelchair and sat down.

'Are you OK?' Tegan directed the question to the Doctor, but it was Nyssa who provided the answer.

'His adrenalin is normalising. It was helping to bridge the synapses.'

The Doctor waved these irrelevances aside with an impatient hand and handed the notebook back to Tegan. 'Sssh—come on, we've got to finish this. About seventeen thousand tons of thrust. Say twenty-five percent of the Architecture.'

'A whole quarter of the TARDIS!' Tegan exclaimed.

Nyssa looked doubtful. 'Which twenty-five percent, Doctor?'

'Doesn't matter . . . same thrust.'

'Oh, that's all right, then,' said Tegan.

The obvious point that had escaped her was picked up sharply by Nyssa. 'It certainly isn't all right. We don't want to jettison the console room.'

'You bet we don't,' said Tegan. 'Not if we're in it!' She turned to the Doctor for his views on the matter, but he appeared to be dozing now. She took him by the shoulder and shook him gently. 'Doctor! Please. One last thing . . .'

The Doctor opened his eyes, and said, as if seeing her for the first time: 'Hello?'

'How do we make sure we don't jettison the console room?' Tegan said slowly, spelling the words out one by one.

The Doctor nodded. 'Ah, yes . . . That's the trouble with manual over-ride. It'll be completely random.'

'Random!' said Nyssa, in something rather louder than her normal tone.

The Doctor lay back in the wheelchair and closed his eyes again. 'Get K9 to explain it to you. Good luck.'

The two girls looked at each other, and then up at the viewer screen, where the stars were closing in rapidly. 'Thanks, Doc,' said Tegan. 'I think we might need it.'

The Master's skin was tight on his face, like a thin mask pulled on over the skull, and the dark eyes had the cruel gleam of gunmetal. 'Well, Adric . . . This is my proposition. Life will immediately become more comfortable for you if you join forces with me. Or do you prefer to remain in the web throughout eternity—a mere utility.'

The boy stared back with what might have been defiance; or perhaps the eyes were glazed with pain and immobility. The Master left him to ponder the question, and the escalator contracted again, returning him to the console. After a moment he touched a switch and turned back to the web. 'You may speak.'

The boy did not respond immediately, but his face betrayed his hesitation as he weighed the temptation. Then, in the hollow voice of defeat, the words came slowly: 'What do you want me to do?'

The thermal protection circuits had dispersed all but the last few wisps of smoke from the room, and now instead of the heat and the air of crisis an atmosphere of deadly stillness prevailed, as if the occupants were crystallised in this final moment of their lives.

Perhaps not all the occupants. Beneath the viewer screen, where the starfield's tightening grip was mercilessly displayed, the Doctor slept peacefully in his wheelchair, oblivious of the tension around him. Nyssa and Tegan stood motionless over the console, their eyes focused on a single red button among the cluster of complicated dials and switches. Presumably it had been there as long as the TARDIS itself, but they had never had cause to notice it before. Now it was the single most important thing in their lives, and the one word engraved on it was engraved on their minds as well. The word was EXECUTE'.

Tegan was the first to break the silence. 'It seems so still now.'

'We've passed the boundary layer. We're moving straight towards the Inrush.' Nyssa glanced down at the calculations she had been making. 'We've got thirty-eight seconds.'

'You make it sound like a scheduled flight to Los Angeles,' exclaimed Tegan. 'How can you keep so calm about it? We're playing Russian roulette with the TARDIS!'

'Thirty-one seconds,' was all Nyssa said.

Tegan looked down at the dangerous red button. 'If I press that it could be the console room we jettison.'

'If?' Nyssa returned the monosyllable with a top-spin of

irony. 'You taught me about "if". As a scientist it's easy to be tyrannised by facts.'

'"If" can work too,' Tegan conceded. 'But I didn't know it would be this chancey.'

'There's no risk at all,' Nyssa said, 'unless you turn the "if" into a fact.' Tegan had to admit that Nyssa had a point. The red button was a dreadful gamble, but the alternative was a certainty. She wasn't sure how or why it had been decided that she should be the one to press the button that either meant escape from the Inrush or the end of her, Nyssa, the Doctor and everything. It was so unfair. Why couldn't the Doctor be the one to do it?

Nyssa was still counting. 'Five seconds . . . four . . .'

Tegan reached for the button, and shut her eyes.

The universe was brilliant with approaching stars that were now as close together as sunbeams dancing on water. Among the dazzling points of light the tiny blue craft sped inconspicuously towards its doom, an oak-leaf riding on a tidal flood.

But nothing is inevitably so; even the fixedest course may change or may be changed. Quite suddenly, the police box became huge, exploding in a flash of dazzling blue light that dimmed the rushing cosmic panorama. The explosion seemed to drain colour and substance from the craft, leaving, as the flash subsided, a ghostly TARDIS image continuing on the same course.

In their inverted time scale the stars drew closer and closer, until they were packed like pebbles on a beach, like grains of sand, like molecules in granite and like the atoms of a diamond.

And then it was Event One, the beginning of everything: a sharp white nothing that blotted out the worlds to come.

5

Jettisoned!

All this was reported to the Master on his viewer screen. He knew nothing of the Doctor's desperate design to escape, and this last and—as far as he was concerned—final glimpse of the TARDIS stirred deep intestinal satisfactions. Above him, on the web, Adric's eyes spoke loudly of his own feelings. But as his hated captor turned back to him, Adric masked his horror with a smile.

'So . . . this petty feud with the Doctor is over, Adric. You are wise to join me.'

The boy met the Master's eyes. 'You've got to keep your side of the bargain.' The Master had given his word that as soon as Adric consented he would release him from the agony of the web. But now as the escalator carried him up to arrange the disconnection of the threads, the Master seemed to be struck by a sudden doubt. As if it drew its power from the mind of its inventor, the device stopped in mid-flight.

'I wonder . . .' said the Master, 'if you are truly sincere? I sense a barrier behind your eyes. You're keeping something from me?'

The boy tried hard to smile back at him. 'How could I.'

'The universe is purged of the Doctor and his impossible dreams of goodness. You and I belong to the future, Adric.'

Adric saw that the Master was watching him closely, testing his reaction. He attempted a nod, but the web constrained his head. 'The Doctor was doomed, I see that now.'

The Master seemed satisfied with the answer. The escalator started up again, extending above the boy's head and bringing him within reach of the suspension points from which the great silvery web hung. As he worked at the business of disconnection, the Master resumed the conversation. 'He might have escaped from the Inrush—yes, even that was possible. But I had in store a trap behind that trap that would have been a joy to spring.'

'Another trap?'

'Of course. The intelligence to plan for contingencies is what distinguishes victors from victims in this great and greedy universe. I had in mind a journey back in time . . . a long waiting . . . Why are you so curious?'

Adric did not answer, but no answer was necessary, because at that moment, just as the Master was in the act of disconnecting one of the threads, a small blue spark made him jump back in surprise. 'Residual voltage in the Hadron Amplifier?' he exclaimed, turning accusingly on the boy. 'You're receiving an image.'

The Master ran down the escalator to the console and spent a moment manipulating the levers. 'What are you concealing from me? Some distant event, beyond the range of my own scanner? I'll burn through your barrier. Bring it to me, boy. Can it possibly be . . .?'

Adric screwed his eyes up tight, fighting against the technology that was pillaging his mind. But once more the Master's voltages overcame his resistance. It appeared on the screen, the image that had begun as a wish and had clarified in his mind to a certainty. The familiar police box shape hung in space, spinning gently against a scattered galaxy of stars.

The Master pulled at a lever on his console and a row of galvanometers kicked into life. His concentration was on the screen, and he ignored the moan of pain from behind him that accompanied the swelling voltages. 'Closer, boy. I must see him . . .'

Up on the web Adric struggled. Though his consciousness was dimmed by the steady drain of the technology, he had begun to realise that he had some measure of control. By an enormous act of will the resistance in his body could constrict the current and drive it back on itself. Now he put everything he could muster into fighting the Master's voltages. Through almost unbearable pain he saw to his satisfaction that the image on the screen was

43

crumbling away.

Adric's wilfulness amused the Master. In anticipation of aeons of co-operation, voluntary or otherwise, he was prepared to tolerate the temporary disobedience. To prevent further damage to his new acquisition, the Master closed a switch on the control panel and the boy slumped into unconsciousness.

'So, Doctor, you have survived,' mused the Master in the silence that followed. 'But at what cost, I wonder . . .'

That very question was occupying the minds of Nyssa and Tegan. For a long time now the Doctor had been sleeping fitfully in the wheelchair, unstirred even by the enormous G-forces released when Tegan had pressed the EXECUTE button. Tegan was searching the data bank to find out what to do next. The only relevant information was that regeneration was a natural process for Time Lords, but there was no advice about what to do when it went wrong . . .

Nyssa bent over the Doctor, concerned at his pasty skin-colour and shallow breathing. 'We must get him straight back to the Zero Room.'

'Wait!' Tegan had found something. 'Ambient complexity is the cause of many of these failures of regeneration,' she read out aloud. 'Some real locations are known to have properties similar to Zero environments, and in some cases are eminently more effective . . .'

Nyssa was beside her at the console. 'That's it. We need to take him somewhere uncomplicated. Somewhere away from technology.' She read on over Tegan's shoulder: 'Classic plainness of surroundings, as exemplified by regions like the Dwellings of Simplicity . . .'

They looked up 'Dwellings of Simplicity' and found the single word 'Castrovalva'.

The Doctor continued dozing inertly in the wheelchair as Nyssa trundled him down the corridor. Apart from the melted lipstick staining the walls the TARDIS showed little sign of the ordeal it had been through. At one point where the lipstick had almost vaporised away she was obliged to stop and check the route. The Doctor stirred, without opening his eyes.

44

'Castro . . . valva . . .' he murmured, savouring the name he must have heard in his sleep.

'That's right,'' said Nyssa, leaning over him. 'The data bank is certain it's the best place to recuperate. It's in Andromeda, a small planet of the Phylox Series . . .'

As if the very name had some recuperative effect, the Doctor opened his eyes. 'And how do we get there?'

'Don't worry, Doctor, Tegan seems to learn very quickly.'

'The air-hostess person's flying it, eh? Well, I wish her the best of luck.' There was a note of impish cynicism in his voice that Nyssa understood only too well. She had her own very pronounced doubts about Tegan's ability; doubts that were justified by the terrible jolting received from time to time as they proceeded on along the corridor.

Tegan was not altogether immune to similar doubts herself, and when Nyssa left her to wheel the Doctor away to the Zero Room the first moments in front of that complicated console had been very frightening. But believing you could do something makes you confident, and confidence brings achievement closer. Tegan didn't mind whether you called it the magic 'if', or—rather more grandly—'recursion'. The idea had helped them survive the Inrush, and she had a feeling it might just get them to the safety of Castrovalva.

Not knowing which to choose from the myriad buttons, levers and handles, Tegan had shut her eyes and groped for whatever instruments came to hand—and the response of the TARDIS was to bank suddenly, throwing her across the room. But when she picked herself up from the floor she was delighted to find that the time column was alight and oscillating.

'That's it!' she exclaimed, 'I've done it! I'm flying the TARDIS!'

The fact that she hadn't and wasn't didn't transpire until very much later.

Navigating the TARDIS is not like navigating a plane; once the co-ordinates are set there is nothing much to do but sit back and worry whether you set them correctly. Another big worry for Tegan was the matter of landing. The Doctor had told her where to find the landing protocol in the data bank, and had gone through it with her quickly, but she knew that when the time came her reactions would have to be tuned to respond immediately. So during the course of the journey she rehearsed the procedure again and again, correcting herself from the small screen of the data bank until she had developed a solid confidence.

Unfortunately, in a way, most of the operations that had to be performed prior to touchdown were taken care of by the TARDIS's infrastructure sub-systems, and there wasn't very much to occupy her mind.

'. . . *on zeroing the co-ordinate differential, automatic systems reactivate the real-world interface, see Main Door, The, Opening of . . .*'

'I hope,' Tegan told herself, 'that it's as simple as it seems.' But she was really rather disappointed that it was so easy.

Her apprehension returned when she saw the approaching planet, a great swirl of emerald mist swimming onto the viewer screen. She knew this had to be where Castrovalva was, because the time column began to slow down of its own accord. From this distance the mysterious verdure of the planet didn't look particularly restful. Tegan imagined rain forests itchy with insects, and wondered if the TARDIS could provide her with Wellington boots.

The time column had chugged to a halt by this time, though it was still alight, indicating that the TARDIS had gone into hover mode. Tegan had to face the fact that it was her task to get the ship and its crew safely down to the planet suspended below them like a mossy tennis ball. She only hoped she could remember the landing procedure . . .

'Hmm . . . Well,' said Tegan to herself, approaching the console and selecting a lever, 'We can't hang about here all day . . .'

Whether she pulled the lever too fast, or in the wrong direction—or indeed whether she had picked the wrong lever altogether—Tegan would never know. The TARDIS gave a sudden stomach-turning swoop and dropped like a stone out of the sky towards the planet below. Tegan was thrown against the wall and held there by the acceleration, unable to reach the console. Perhaps this was just as well, because the TARDIS automatic circuits were able to take over, and helped to cushion the landing.

Nevertheless, the jolt was terrifying as the travel-weary Type 40 hit the planet surface.

Tegan picked herself up from the floor, which was now leaning over at a crazy angle, and her first thought was for the Doctor. The bump had shaken her badly, so what had it done to him in his fragile state? And then she remembered that he and Nyssa would probably not have felt anything at all in the Zero Room, which had its own local gravity.

In fact the rough landing did shake the Doctor, and saved his life. Nyssa had followed the smeary red trail back to the Zero Room without much difficulty. The big double doors were slightly ajar, just as the Doctor had left them in his haste to join in and help. But when Nyssa pushed them open she discovered to her horror that there was no opening behind them—just a continuation of the TARDIS wall.

She couldn't believe her eyes. She pulled both doors open wide and thumped her fists against the roundels, but the wall was completely solid. Hearing a faint grunt behind her, she turned to see that the Doctor, still slumped in his chair, had lifted his head to take in the situation. 'Jettisoned!' he hissed through his teeth.

Of course! Nyssa should have grasped that immediately. The Zero Room had gone, as part of the random quarter of the TARDIS they had burned up to get out of the Inrush.

But a theoretical understanding of what had happened was not much comfort, and certainly no solution. Nyssa tried to rack her brains, but her mind was as blank as the wall itself. The Doctor was fumbling for something in his inside coat pocket. He brought out a long silvery device, about the size of a large ballpoint pen, with a small reflector at the end.

Nyssa recognised the sonic screwdriver, but had no idea what the Doctor expected her to do with it.

Her question irritated him. 'What do you think you do with a screwdriver? Unscrew the door hinges. If you wouldn't mind . . .'

She started on the left-hand door. The dull silvery metal was

47

surprisingly light for the size of the door, but there was enough of its great bulk to drag on the heads of the screws as she undid them. The top screws were too high to reach, until she had the idea of borrowing the wheelchair to use as a sort of precarious step-ladder.

A desultory conversation with the Doctor accompanied the work. He kept dozing off and then jerking awake again with some irritating bit of advice, or a completely irrelevant observation. He wouldn't answer her main question, even though she kept putting it to him in different forms.

'But this won't get us into the Zero Room, Doctor. It's gone. We burnt it up.' She wanted to ask: So what is the point of all this unscrewing? But she didn't want to seem unwilling to help.

'Doors and hinges,' muttered the Doctor, slumped in the corner of the corridor where she had been obliged to deposit him while she commandeered the wheelchair. 'It's an open-and-shut case.'

She had to concentrate completely on the door as she removed the last hinge, because all the weight was pulling on one screw. Eventually she manoeuvred the door into a position where it was leaning against the wall. She was about to tackle the second door when she noticed the Doctor's head had almost completely disappeared into his coat collar. She knelt down beside him and turned his face to the light. The pastiness of complexion had begun to take on a bluish tinge.

'Cyanosis!' she exclaimed under her breath. 'We must do something quickly!'

She wasn't quite sure who she meant by 'we'—there were only herself and the Doctor, with Tegan away at the end of miles of corridor. 'I must do something,' she corrected. But it didn't sound quite right: if there were a solution waiting to be found she and the Doctor would have to find it together, because by herself she hadn't the faintest idea what to do. The Doctor knew; somewhere in that heap of crumpled flannel were worlds of wisdom. But he seemed to be slipping away into an ever-deepening coma, taking the knowledge with him.

Nyssa put her lips to his ear and whispered: 'Doctor! Please! What do I do next?'

His skin was a pale, transparent blue now, and he seemed to

be growing thinner by the minute inside the cream-coloured coat.

'There's no way into the Zero Room, Doctor. It's gone . . . What do we do?'

That was the moment that, far away in the console room, Tegan chose to pull the lever intending to bring the TARDIS in to land. The almighty lurch that followed hurled Nyssa across the corridor, and at the same time the loose Zero Room door slipped from the wall where she had leant it, wavered uncertainly for a moment, then toppled, careering down towards the Doctor.

Nyssa heard the heavy thud and scrambled to her feet, expecting to see the Doctor flattened by the impact. But instead, by a miracle, the loose door had slammed into the opposite wall only centimetres above his head and jammed diagonally across the corridor, forming a sort of triangular lean-to with the Doctor underneath it. Nyssa went down on her hands and knees and peeked under the sloping roof made by the door. Partially enclosed by whatever substance it was that gave the Zero Room its unique qualities, the Doctor's pale face smiled back at her. He was still weak, but already visibly revived.

'Yes, yes, that's the idea,' he said delightedly. 'We'll make our own Zero Room with what's left.'

Tegan breathed deeply. After the characterless atmosphere of the TARDIS the air smelled sharp and clean, breezing against her face as she stood on a grassy knoll surveying the countryside. In front of her wild shrubland rolled down to a muddy stream. Further off the terrain seemed strangely convoluted, with tree-lined hills folding into themselves as far as the eye could see. Although not quite the sinister planet she had imagined, it was certainly untamed, and might even be dangerous, for the deep green foliage could house any number of unmentionable creatures.

The birdsong was reassuring; liquid melody flowed up from the woods, calming her fears. To get a better view she strolled back to the TARDIS, where it lay half-buried in the ground, tilted over about twenty degrees to the vertical, as if half-heartedly pretending to be a small blue pyramid. Touchdown had not been quite up to CAA standards, she had to admit, but a landing was a landing. The main problem had been getting out through the door, and she was grateful to whoever had designed the TARDIS for having the good sense to make the doors open inwards, otherwise her efforts would have been completely fruitless.

She hauled herself up the sloping wall and climbed onto the roof. It did cross her mind that perhaps she ought to be helping Nyssa with the Doctor, but the fresh air tempted her to postpone the prospect of descending back into the TARDIS. There is such a thing as a surfeit of corridors.

In any case, there was work to be done out here. Nyssa would want a report on the surface conditions, and it would certainly be a help to have some idea in which direction the Dwellings of Simplicity lay. From the top of the TARDIS she could see no signs of habitation. But half a mile away, along the grassy ridge that ran parallel to the river, a very tall tree promised a commanding view of the landscape. She was sure Castrovalva would be somewhere in sight of its top branches.

The spring-like sunshine and the marvellous clarity of the birdsong calmed her fears about wild creatures, and Tegan set off on a recce of the terrain.

6

The Quest for Castrovalva

Nyssa made two complete journeys from the Zero Room to the console room, transporting the doors one by one. The aluminium struts of the wheelchair reminded her with a constant protestation of creaks that they were hardly designed to take that sort of weight, but luckily they held out. When she went back to fetch the Doctor the blueness and the shortness of breath had returned. She picked him up (he seemed to weigh hardly anything), bundled him into the wheelchair and raced back to the console room at a breakneck speed that threatened to spill him out at every corner. Perhaps it was a peculiarity of the TARDIS architecture, or another of those psychological phenomena, but the distance between the console room and the Zero Room seemed, luckily, to be shrinking with familiarity, and she was able to restore the Doctor to the shelter of one of the doors before his condition became serious again.

While he recovered Nyssa propped the other door against the console and began to assemble the ion bonder she had brought with her from Traken. It was a small device comprising a probe and a handgrip, and she carried the two parts in separate pockets for safety. With a deft twist of her fingers they came together; then she touched a button and a fierce blue light sprang from the tip of the instrument. She adjusted a knob until the light was barely visible and applied it to the door. Her hands were shaking from the exertion of all that transportation, so the line she drew wasn't as straight as she would have liked. The dull silver metal glowed in the wake of the instrument, spluttering up little rivulets of larva as she moved it slowly from the top of the door

51

to the bottom. Then, with a snapping sound, the door split neatly into two halves.

It took a long time to cut the door into sections of the right size, and welding the parts together again at right-angles was even trickier. During the work it occurred to her to wonder what had happened to Tegan, not that Tegan could have been very helpful as there was only one ion bonder, and you needed a good deal of skill and judgement to use it.

Once the construction was partially assembled she tried to carry the Doctor over to it, but he had recovered most of his proper weight, and objected wordlessly at being moved. It took a lot of diplomacy and brute force from Nyssa to get him to climb inside—and the whole idea had been the Doctor's in the first place. This was the 'open-and-shut case' he had been mumbling about, a kind of modestly proportioned sarcophagus built from all that remained of the Zero Room.

When she came back to him with the rough-cut shape cannibalised from the second door to form the lid, she was very pleased to see him smiling. If only his eyes had been open she felt sure they would have had something of the old twinkle in them.

'I'm sorry about the box,' she said lamely, as though it were her fault. 'It looks very small, Doctor.'

She hardly expected him to reply. But his lips moved and he whispered: 'And unlike the TARDIS—it is very small. Eh?' He cackled faintly, inviting her to join in the joke. And then he said, in a rather stronger voice: 'And don't call it a box. Very constricting little word. Call it a cabinet. That's it . . . the Zero Cabinet.'

At that moment Tegan slid in through the door, bouncing with confidence. 'OK, the travel arrangements are all organised. There's not far to go, anyway.'

'To Castrovalva?' said Nyssa. 'You've seen it.'

'Shinned up a tree. And it's an afternoon's walk from here. More or less.'

Nyssa waved towards the Zero Cabinet. 'We've got to carry the Doctor, don't forget.'

'Just the Zero Cabinet.' The voice came from inside the Cabinet, although the Doctor still had his eyes shut.

Tegan leant over him. 'What's that, Doc?'

'You won't feel my weight,' said the voice. 'I'll make it easy for you. I'll be levitating.'

Perhaps 'easy' wasn't the word for it, but in comparison with the rest of their adventures so far the business of setting off with the Doctor on the route to Castrovalva was fraught only with minor problems. The first appeared when Nyssa had finished fashioning the lid, sealed it down over the Doctor and with Tegan's help was carrying the Cabinet through the exit. Of all the calculations Nyssa had made in assembling the Zero Cabinet, she had not remembered to measure the real world interface of the TARDIS—the police-box doors. If the Cabinet had been a centimetre wider the result could have been a disastrous delay, but with much pulling from Nyssa and more pushing from Tegan, they just managed to squeeze out into the open air.

Despite the Doctor's promises to levitate, the box itself felt rather heavy. Nyssa disappeared back into the TARDIS and returned with the wheelchair. As the two girls lifted the Cabinet onto it Tegan suddenly stopped. 'Ssh . . . It's the Doctor. He's tapping on the lid. He wants to say something.'

'It can't be,' said Nyssa. 'The Cabinet's supposed to be like a miniature Zero Room. You wouldn't hear him tapping.'

'You mean we have to open the lid to communicate with him?'

'We can't even do that. Once the lid's closed the material is self-fusing. Only the Doctor can open it from inside.' Nyssa hesitated. 'At least, that's how it's supposed to be . . .'

Apparently the Doctor did want to communicate, because their departure was further delayed by the lid sliding open a little way, to reveal the Doctor's face, which looked paler than ever in the sunshine.

He opened his eyes and attempted a smile.

Nyssa bent over him. 'What is it, Doctor . . .?'

He blinked in the light. 'I just wanted to say . . .'

'Yes?' Tegan drew closer too.

'Er . . . Forgotten. Never mind, plenty of time . . . It'll come to me.'

The sunlight seemed to be hurting his eyes, so Nyssa began to draw the lid shut. Then he blinked rapidly and said in a tremulous voice: 'No, no . . . Remembered. Thank you. Wanted to say thank you.'

The girls put the lid back into place, Nyssa started up the battery-driven motor on the wheelchair, and they set off along the ridge that ran above the stream.

One other small problem emerged at this point, and if they had been older and wiser they might have seen in it an omen of the terrible events to come. But as anyone arriving on a new planet knows, it is proverbially easy to mistake features of the landscape. Tegan's simple recipe for the journey was to find the tree she had climbed and travel from there in a bee-line towards the small white townscape she had sighted on the distant hill. This would almost certainly be Castrovalva, there being no other town on the planet according to the TARDIS data base.

The problem was, Tegan couldn't find the tree.

The town, according to Tegan's sighting (and she was sure she hadn't been dreaming) was on the other side of the river, quite a long way upstream. It seemed sensible to continue along the ridge until they found what looked like a good crossing place. The going was good; the sunshine and mild air were rapidly dispelling the accumulated claustrophobia of the TARDIS, and with the motorised wheelchair the transport of the Doctor became a very simple procedure.

When Tegan thought they had gone far enough she pointed diagonally across the stream. 'I definitely saw it. More that way, I think.'

The bank was steep in places, and as they descended they discovered treacherous muddy patches, so that while Nyssa steered, Tegan had to hold on to the Zero Cabinet to keep it perched on the wheelchair. As they got nearer the stream it became harder and harder to control the load, and the wheelchair began to drag them down the slope.

''Strewth, look out!' Tegan shouted. 'The Doctor!' The Cabinet was starting to run away with them, but as they grabbed at it the wheelchair tumbled away from under it, turned round and began racing backwards towards the stream.

They put the Cabinet down and heard a splash from below. Nyssa ran down after the chair, but it was too late; when she got to the bottom of the bank it was cutting a V of white spume in midstream, upside down, with a wheel missing. What was worse, Nyssa tried to stop too suddenly, slipped on the mud, tripped and fell in after it.

When they looked back on that long journey to Castrovalva they both agreed that the crossing of the stream marked a turning point. They had set out in high spirits, to the accompaniment of sunlight and birdsong. The sunlight and birdsong continued on the other side of the stream, but other elements began to creep in: mud, weariness, brambles and frustration.

The opposite bank was welcoming at first, and thick with grass and flowers. Tegan found a dry spot, and lay on her stomach to cup her hands into the clear water and cool her face. The Zero Cabinet lay in the long grass beside her.

'Are you sure I can't give you a hand,' she called out, leaning her face back to dry it in the sun. Behind her a suggestion of a path ran alongside the stream. They had hauled the wheelchair up there, and Nyssa, still damp from her rescue efforts, was crouched beside it, checking it over.

'No, it's all right.' Nyssa had managed to salvage the other wheel; replacing that would be simple enough. But the one that had remained attached to the axle was badly warped, and what was needed was some dexterous re-dimensioning. Tegan was a willing enough helper, if impetuous at times, but the job needed technological skill, and the ion bonder.

Nyssa drew the two halves of the instrument from her tunic, assembled them, and pointed the probe at the wheel. Nothing happened. She shook it doubtfully, flicked open a catch in the handgrip, and a trickle of water dribbled from the mechanism.

A rather unscientific oath escaped her lips. The wetting had shorted out the power packs, and the replacements were back in the TARDIS. She stowed the device away and walked over to where Tegan was sunning herself. 'We'll have to carry him from now on. The wheelchair's finished.'

Above the path rose a stretch of shrubbery, where the dense rubbery leaves and yellow flowers the size of small cabbages might provide cover for any number of the wild animals Tegan had feared. But the two girls were at that moment too concerned with the loss of the wheelchair and organising themselves for the further portage of the Zero Cabinet to pay any further attention to the vegetation. Even if they had, it is not likely, with all the general rustle and sway of the leaves in the wind which was now rising, that they would have noticed one particular branch being drawn slightly aside, as a hand parted the foliage. From the hassaradra bush, Ruther's warrior scout, in the majestic garb of the hunt, gazed down upon the two visitors.

With the abandoning of the wheelchair, the quest for Castrovalva became a struggle. The path, such as it was, soon petered out and they found themselves carrying the Zero Cabinet through weeds that snagged at their clothing. The strain was beginning to show in Nyssa's voice when she said: 'Are you sure this is the right way?'

The trees grew denser here, and were closing in over their heads. 'It had better be!' said Tegan, trying to put a good face on it. But as they struggled deeper into the wood even the exotic call of the birds seemed to take on sinister overtones. There were brambles and thorn bushes everywhere now, and the ground beneath their feet had become muddy and uncertain.

The wood went on for a long time, and all the while the Doctor seemed to be getting heavier and heavier. Tegan's apologies lost their breeziness, until she had run out of ways of saying sorry. She even began to wonder if the tall tree by the river, and the view from the top branches, had been a dream after all.

Eventually they came upon a patch of drier ground where it seemed safe to put the cabinet down and collapse onto a nearby log. 'Sorry . . .' said Tegan for the umteenth time. 'I was sure it was this way.'

She rummaged in her flightbag to find some consolation—a piece of chewing-gum, perhaps, or even just a mirror, so that she could look at her face and reassure herself that she was Tegan Jovanka, and not just some forgotten fragment of somebody else's nightmare. She found two lipstick dispensers, but they were empty, their contents having been dispersed along the TARDIS corridors. Nevertheless, she managed to scoop out a smidgin from the base of one of them. Unfolding the small round mirror and propping it on a branch in front of her, she raised her red-daubed little finger to her face.

It never reached her lips. A breeze shifted the alignment of the mirror at that moment, replacing the reflection of her face in the silver frame with a glimpse of a huge white hill that rose up beyond the trees behind her. It was not the hill itself that made her mouth drop open with surprise, although she had until now received no hint that the edge of the wood was close. But surmounting the blanched rocks that formed the summit, outlined sharply against the deepening blue of the sky, was a neat townscape fringed with walls and turrets that fluttered with coloured flags.

'Castrovalva!' She turned round and stared up through the tree-tops: it was not a dream. But in her excitement she brushed against the mirror, which tumbled from its perch and shattered unnoticed against the log. If she had turned to the mirror now she would have seen in it the image of that hill-top town broken into tiny fragments, a warning of the worst that was to come.

But it was not a moment for reflection, and the mirror lay forgotten. The sight of Castrovalva had revived the spirits of the two friends, and now was a time for action and quick decisions. The two girls plucked up handfuls of bracken and broke off branches, then Tegan left Nyssa to cover up the Cabinet while she recced the route out of the wood.

When she came back, the Doctor was well hidden beneath the camouflage. 'It's a very steep hill—seems to be rough rocks all the way up. But people obviously live there, so there must be a path to it.'

Nyssa put the finishing touches to the camouflage. 'All right, let's find it.'

'You're sure it's all right to leave him?' asked Tegan.

Nyssa explained again about the strong force interaction sealing the internal interface. 'Nothing can open this Cabinet unless the Doctor wants it opened.'

'I'll take your word for it.' Tegan was impatient to go. 'Come on. It'll be night before we know it.'

As the two girls moved off a nearby tree-branch stirred, shifted by an unseen hand. Once more watching eyes noted their departure, and then the stalker turned and, with the silent motion of the hunter, retreated into the undergrowth.

The wood suddenly debouched into broad sunlight at the foot of the great white hill. The two friends skirted the rough terrain, clambering upwards until they came on a narrow path among the rocks, which ran like an old scar through the chalky landscape until is disappeared around the jagged profile of the hill.

They paused to catch their breath and debate whether to continue their investigations or go back for the Doctor. Nyssa pointed out that the path might well come to nothing, just as the one by the river had done. There would be no point in carrying the Doctor this far only to arrive at a dead end, so they explored a little further.

As it turned out, Nyssa's caution was well founded. The path began to ascend too steeply for comfort. Soon it was running beside a dangerous cliff whose ragged edge drew closer and closer to the sheer rock wall until the track they were following was squeezed between the two into nothing but a giddying view of the countryside below.

Tegan craned her head to look up at the white-walled town. 'There's got to be some way into this place.'

'We need the Doctor's help,' said Nyssa. 'We'll just have to go back.'

'We could certainly use some advice,' Tegan agreed. 'But how do we get in touch with him through the Zero interface?'

'We just have to sit and wait until he decides to open the lid,' said Nyssa, in the special matter-of-fact voice she reserved for alarming statements of that kind. 'Come on . . .'

But a lot had happened while they were away. The girls had not been gone long from where the Zero Cabinet nestled under its camouflage in the wood when there were whispering voices in the undergrowth again. 'And this is where you saw them?' asked one.

The other nodded, and the blood-coloured feathers that fringed the tall headmask shivered against the leaves.

'Mergrave must be told of this,' said the first speaker, whose attire was gaudier still, for in addition to the war mask he was wrapped in a robe of purple silk shot through with gold. A susurration in the undergrowth betrayed the presence of other warriors around them.

The gathered huntsmen had not yet noticed the heap of branches and bracken that concealed the Zero Cabinet. Even so, it was not the best time for the Doctor to choose to unhitch the lid and edge it open. A pair of much refreshed eyes twinkled out at the world from beneath the camouflage.

Nyssa sensed there was something wrong with the Cabinet the moment she began to pull off the bunches of branches. Tegan had hung back a little way off, her eye caught by something on the ground, and Nyssa decided to say nothing until she was sure. She touched the lid and it wobbled slightly. The Cabinet was open.

Tegan suddenly straightened up from her examination of the grass. 'Blood!' she exclaimed, waving across to Nyssa. There was a red stain on her fingers.

But Nyssa had no time to listen, for she had lifted back the lid and was staring into the empty interior of the Zero Cabinet.

'He's gone!' she called out in a hollow voice. 'The Doctor's gone.'

7

Within the Walls

Nyssa and Tegan were alone without the Doctor on a strange planet. In spite of his weakness and his wandering mind, just having him with them had given the two friends a sort of strength. Now they could do nothing but stare into the empty Cabinet, feeling a deep inner emptiness of their own.

Nyssa tried to be reassuring, but her voice was small and uncertain. 'The Doctor must have opened it himself. Nobody else could have done it. So it must have worked, the Zero effect. He must be feeling better.'

Tegan tore a leaf from a tree and wiped the blood from her fingers. 'Until whatever happened . . . happened. We've got to find him.' Her eye followed the gruesome trail of red stains in the grass for as far as she could see. It ran towards the great hill surmounted by walls and turrets, and Tegan found the name forming slowly under her breath: 'Castrovalva!' The sun was sinking lower in the sky, and in the yellowing light the small town took on a less friendly aspect.

'And the data bank said it was going to be so simple!' said Nyssa, as they set off towards it, following the trail.

But then, just as they were passing beneath one of the squat trees that edged the wood, with hardly a sound except the rush of air and the rustle of foliage, a sudden horrifying stream of silver cloth and feathers dropped down onto them. They started back at the sight of the tall hollow-eyed mask that confronted them, but before the two girls had time to catch their breath a crowd of other warriors had sprung up from the bushes.

'Run!' shouted Tegan, and they headed back into the woods,

darting in and out of the low trees like frightened fish among coral. From behind them, puzzlingly, came no sound of pursuit, but they did not dare to look over their shoulders. Then, when they had run their lungs out, they dived into a clump of bracken and lay low.

In the woods around them nothing stirred. After a moment Tegan's head reappeared above the green fronds . . . and then Nyssa's. 'They're playing cat-and-mouse with us,' Tegan whispered.

'Whoever "they" are.' Cautiously the two girls stood up, and Nyssa went on urgently: 'We've got to find the Doctor. Until he's properly regenerated he's terribly vulnerable.' Together, scanning suspicious-looking trees for any hint of movement, they made their way back towards the Zero Cabinet to pick up the blood trail.

It happened that at that moment the Doctor was lying unmoving on a flat patch of rocky ground on the far side of the big white hill where Castrovalva perched. Here the trail of blood showed more distinctly on the bare ochre soil, running in crimson splashes almost towards the point where the Doctor lay. Almost, but not quite, for it missed the Doctor's head by several feet, running on towards a winding road, hardly more than a wide, well-trodden path, that turned upwards towards the lofty townlet.

The Doctor opened one eye—he had closed them both to listen more intently to the ground, Indian fashion—and now squinted through the few tufts of grass in the direction taken by the trail. After a moment he sat up, gazing into the distance.

'Hmmm . . .' he hummed to himself. 'Twelve of them at least. War party, maybe.' And, with a child-like unconcern for the dangers, he set off after them.

The two girls were only too aware of danger. It didn't help that the wood was so misleading, unfolding corrals of open ground from time to time that made you think you were at the edge of it, only to wrap its thick foliage around you again as you stumbled on. Then suddenly, without ever coming across the place where they had left the Zero Cabinet, Nyssa and Tegan were grateful to find themselves returned to the wide sweep of the landscape, confronting the hill of Castrovalva.

As luck would have it, they had found the Doctor too. Looking up, they saw the small figure clambering uncertainly high among the rocks. 'Perhaps he's found the way in?' said Tegan, as the pair of them hurried off after him.

In fact the Doctor had only the distant glimmer of an idea about where he was going—something deep and instinctive was driving him upwards towards Castrovalva. Occasionally he stopped to examine the blood trail, and his eyes would wander over the edge of the path and down the steep hill to the hungry white teeth of the rocks below him. But apart from the giddiness he remained unaware of the danger. His mind was filled with subliminal images of other dizzying heights: flashes of girders and gantries shaped like a great bowl in the sky, from which someone he had once known well was swinging on a single cable that stretched and snapped strand by strand.

A mêlée of echoing voices seemed to be calling 'Doctor'; voices from the past and from the future jangling together in a desperate cachophony. He was not to know that among the confusion of sounds in his mind were the real shouts of Tegan and Nyssa blown on the wind from far below. 'Doctor!' the voices called, all of them, in a ragged chorus, and he realised that he too was calling the Doctor, that he needed him urgently, and that somewhere among the white walls that crested the hill he might stand a chance of finding him.

Further up the steepening path at a place the Doctor had yet to reach the way was blocked by a sheer rock wall. Here the warriors in their wild attire paused, huddled around some large burden they had set down on the ground. One warrior with a mask that was taller than the rest, even allowing for its magnificent crest of peacock feathers, unwrapped his arm from the gaudy cloth of red, blue and gold that hung about his shoulders, and held up his hand for general silence.

'Once again we wait for Ruther,' announced the imposing figure in a booming voice. 'Was there ever a man with such capacity to lose both his quarry and himself?' The rhetorical question was greeted with a ripple of laughter.

The merriment died down again, giving way to the sound of the sharpening and cleaning of the many weapons of the hunt that the warriors carried. The sun had become a trembling orange globe touching the horizon when, unseen by the gathering, the Doctor's face appeared above a nearby rock. Curiosity fought with caution in his confused mind, but some instinct for survival made him duck down out of sight again.

But hiding and waiting did not at all match his restless mood. A sense of the quest was forming in him—although, like all the best quests, he had only the vaguest idea what it was he was seeking. It had something to do with the personality called the Doctor, with whom he had a vague connection, like a long-lost cousin. And these strangely apparelled savages, dangerous though they might look (and indeed be), were destined somehow to lead him to his goal.

He began to scout behind the cover of the rocks. His concentration, in his lucid moments every bit as sharp as the knives and spears that gleamed in the light of the sinking sun, was so drawn into trying to see what it was the war party was crowding around that he failed to notice a second group approaching up the hill behind him. It was the long-awaited Ruther, whose scout had first spotted the arrival of strangers on the planet. At last, hearing the sound of footfalls, the Doctor turned round to find the magnificent figures of yet more warriors fencing the sky behind him.

Instinct rather than natural courtesy drew the Doctor to his feet. He backed away awkwardly over the rocks—and found himself among the group he had been watching.

Ruther was pointing at him. 'This is another Stranger.'

Like Ruther's, the voice of the warrior who had been waiting was hollow and sinister behind the tall mask. 'Who are you, Stranger?'

'That, my feathered friends,' said the Doctor, 'is the strangest thing of all. D'you know, I'm not entirely sure.'

Only scores of feet below, though many times further by way of the path, Nyssa and Tegan had been given early warning of the danger closing in on the Doctor from behind. They had concealed themselves as best they could in the shadow of a boulder, helpless as they watched the late-arriving group carry past a familiar object on their shoulders. 'No wonder we couldn't find it,' exclaimed Nyssa under her breath. It was the Zero Cabinet.

They let the warriors go by, and resumed the struggle up the path, their lengthening shadows alternately trailing and scouting ahead as they wound to and fro up the hillside. Any moment they might be discovered, but they knew the Doctor was in urgent need of their help.

Then from the rocks above them, frightening them out of their skins, came the penetrating shriek of a hunting horn. Tegan, whose reactions were faster, pulled Nyssa against the cliff wall, where they pressed themselves into the shadows, feeling sure they must have been seen. But instead of cries of pursuit there came a terrible rumbling sound. The solid rock itself began to shake, and they had to clutch at the sparse dry foliage to stop themselves falling.

It was not an earthquake that opened the hillside, the Doctor was gratified to see, but some huge concealed mechanism that levered back an expanse of the vertical cliff face to reveal a long flight of steps leading up inside the rock. The sun was no more than a fading red stain on the horizon, but the flambeaux that were being lit held back the enclosing blanket of darkness, and flashed sparkles of light from the cave walls.

The tall masked leader who had waited for the one called Ruther raised up a hand to his warriors, gesturing that the Doctor should be the first to ascend the steps. The bearers of the burden that had been the centre of interest before the Doctor's arrival picked up their load and went in behind him, followed closely by Ruther's group with their prize of the Zero Cabinet.

Nyssa and Tegan had overcome their fear and run the last few steps of the way to see what was happening. They arrived just as the straggling tail of the torch-lit procession disappeared into the cavernous entrance. Unthinkingly the two girls ran forward. 'Doctor! Come back!' they shouted together, but their voices were drowned under the sound of the rock entrance closing once more, blending into the cliff wall and leaving them in a sudden darkness.

The Doctor lost all track of the geography of his journey, but the steps at last gave way to even ground, and he found himself standing on flagstones under a star-bright sky. Shadowy buildings fringed the wide square, in the centre of which was a fountain. Beside it a great spit had been set up, with a pile of wood beneath it ready to be lit.

They seated him on a bench that backed up to the fountain. The bustle and merriment around him came to his ears as a confusion of sound, but he could make out the hollow masked voices of his captors clearly enough.

'Shall I instruct the women to light the fire?' asked Ruther of his taller masked companion.

'We'll wait for Shardovan,' said the other, and then, addressing the warriors in general: 'Well, sirs, today has been a good adventure in the Wilds beyond the Walls.'

Several voices responded in assent, and among them the Doctor heard: 'And a quarry worth the name.' At this the one called Ruther intruded a note of scepticism. 'A fair kill, though I have seen better.'

A new voice, tinged with deep melancholy, joined the exchange. 'Ah, if we could cook your memories, Ruther, we would feast indeed.'

At that moment women were putting torches to the bonfire, and the flames that sprang up beneath the spit seemed to join in the general merriment at the newcomer's remark. The Doctor raised his head at the sound of the new voice, and in the firelight thought he saw a tall, slim, distinguished gentleman in dark, plain suiting and a spotless high-collared shirt. Had he been in his right mind the incongruity would have come as a great surprise, but the Big Dipper of the Doctor's consciousness was in the middle of one of its low swoops, and the part of his mind that retained a measure of control was sure he must be hallucinating.

The newcomer bent to look at the Doctor. Disappointed possibly at the air of vagueness in the eyes that met his, he said over his shoulder, not unpleasantly: 'I trust, Mergrave, you have returned from the hunt with something more edible than this lifeless unfortunate?' The Doctor took in the words, though their meaning escaped him, and he did not at all catch the reply from Mergrave, the hunt leader. The dark-suited gentleman turned back to the Doctor with a strange gleam in his eye, although it may simply have been a trick of the firelight. 'You are fit for dinner, sir I trust?'

Tegan shivered. A cold wind had begun to gust around the rock face producing a curious moaning sound that very much matched her own mood. Nyssa, who always seemed capable of working on without complaint under any sort of adversity, was paying patient attention to where she guessed the great door fitted into the rock.

'Closed without a trace!' she announced eventually. 'If we had a three-micron beam wedge . . .'

'Well, we haven't,' Tegan snapped. The cold and the frustration were getting to her.

Nyssa remained calm. 'I said "if". You taught me about "if", remember.'

'It's not that soft of "if". It's what we can do with what we've got—*if* we only used a bit of initiative.' Despite her despondence, Tegan had been surveying the possibilities of climbing the cliff. The white turrets, visible in the starlight, didn't seem all that far away.

She signalled to Nyssa to give her a leg up. The rock was not as smooth as it looked, and there were easy handholds if you felt around for them. She found a convenient ledge and reached down for Nyssa's hand. That was how, without making any particular decision to do it, they found themselves engaged in the perilous ascent of the rock face.

They climbed for a long time, but the white walls of Castrovalva still seemed as far above them as ever. 'We'll never get up there,' said Nyssa, stating it as a fact.

'Do you want to go back?' asked Tegan.

Nyssa glanced down at the path below, which was now no more than a thin silver thread in the moonlight. The return journey looked even more perilous. 'We seem to be committed.'

From his position on the bench in the square the Doctor was beginning to see a little sense, and what he saw he did not like. For the past few minutes his still-confused consciousness had been wrestling with three disparate perceptions: the hunting

66

garb his captors wore, the cooking arrangements being made so close by, and his own involuntary presence among them. In the light of the fires that were now flickering under the empty spit, the masked faces that loomed over him took on a spurious liveliness. They looked hungry, these savages, and the Doctor saw an awful ambiguity in this invitation to dinner.

The mysteriously sober figure in the midst of all that tribal splendour eyed the Doctor across the large oak table. The gaze was sharp and intelligent, though not especially friendly, and the Doctor found nothing particularly reassuring about it.

The warrior whose name was Mergrave spoke from behind his mask. 'We should inform the Portreeve of our unusual catch.'

The sober figure nodded. 'That has been done. But not his purpose here. May one know that?'

'He says he doesn't know who he is, or why he has come,' said Mergrave. The besuited man learned across the table towards the Doctor. 'I admire an individual with an open mind. My own, I fear, is closed upon the opinion that I am Shardovan.' The elegantly cuffed hand extended itself across the table towards the Doctor, who shook it automatically. 'I have the honour to be Librarian to the Dwellings of Castrovalva.'

The Doctor's eyes sharpened. 'Librarian? Books and stuff?'

Shardovan smiled wanly. 'Books are the principal business of a library, sir.'

'Then you read?' the Doctor remarked, turning to take in all the warriors. 'You all read?'

The general amusement at the Doctor's surprise broke up as a crowd of bustling women arrived on the scene. Some came forward with food to set on the table, while others helped divest Mergrave, Ruther and the other warriors of their ferocious outer wrappings. Soon, to the Doctor's added astonishment, they stood in front of him without masks, in clothes as conventional as those of the Librarian.

The hunt leader had been transformed into a jovial, balding gentleman who without the added elevation of the tall mask, turned out to be rather on the short side. He introduced himself as Mergrave, and continued. 'We read too much, in my opinion. There is in this town of Castrovalva, sir, a general dedication to bodily inertia that quite defies description.'

The continued efforts of the women had by this time covered the table with the makings of a sizeable banquet. The mysterious burden the huntsmen had carried all the way up from the woods proved to be a wild pig of enormous proportions, and this delicious prize was set up to barbecue on the rotating spit over the fire. Warming at a more comfortable distance in its flames and cooled by a fine mist that wafted occasionally from the fountain, the Doctor sat back in his chair smiling. 'Castrovalva. Yes . . . I remember now. The place to rest . . .'

The warrior called Ruther had by now removed his own mask to reveal the mildly myopic expression of a man who might be a bank clerk. 'And rest you shall, sir. Some refreshment, and then we must show you to your quarters.' He reached out for a goblet that had been put before the Doctor and filled it from a jug. Ruther raised his glass in a toast, which the Doctor was about to return when he spotted a jar of fresh celery that had just been put down in the middle of the table. He tweaked out a stick, tapped Ruther's glass with it, and sank his teeth into it with a satisfying crunch.

'Definitely civilisation,' said the Doctor with a broad smile of satisfaction.

8

The Dark Reflection

After a few more sticks of celery the Doctor's appetite was satisfied, although the preparations for the meal were still to be completed. The rotating pig had begun to take on a crisp brown colour, wafting succulent smells over to the table where they sat. But the Gallifreyan temperament tends to see the world from the other person's point of view: the Castrovalvans were looking forward to their feast, as well they might after all the hard work they had put into it, but the Doctor's natural sympathies lay with the pig, which was not coming out of this at all well.

Reluctant to offend his hosts he told them with perfect truth that he was feeling very tired. Mergrave tapped his nose in a knowing way, and jumped up, saying he had just the thing for the occasion. The Doctor chewed one more stick of celery, in order not to disappear in too much haste, then he allowed Ruther to conduct him to the quarters that were already being prepared for him.

Shardovan came with them, and as they mounted the steps that led up to a terrace of small dwelling places replied to a question the Doctor had put to him earlier. 'I understand your natural puzzlement in the matter of our outdoor garments. The cause of all this is Mergrave, sir. He has devised a religion he calls "Exercise".'

'In pursuit of which belief,' added Ruther, 'he drives us to hunt animals in the Wilds beyond the Walls.'

The Doctor nodded. 'The hunt! Yes.' Some of the history of his arrival there was coming back to him. He remembered white rocks and blood, but when he tried to think back beyond that time there was only an uneasy nothingness. He turned to Shardovan. 'You weren't at the hunt.'

'Alas, no,' said Shardovan, in a sardonic tone that conveyed no particular trace of regret. They had reached an arched porch, and now Shardovan turned the handle of a door that opened into a pleasant stone-walled room lit by a single lantern.

Mergrave was already in the room, mixing a glass of liquid. As they entered, Ruther settled himself in a chair, and said good-humouredly: 'Shardovan was detained by being longer in the body than the available habiliments could match.'

'The garments with which we stir our courage to the hunt,' explained Shardovan, 'are relics of our ancestors. A smaller breed of men, who, as I believe, wore down their stature with too much hunting. You will notice that I am tall.'

'I suppose that's why they made you Librarian,' suggested the Doctor, 'reaching down books from the top shelf.'

The Castrovalvans enjoyed this remark, although the Doctor in his confused state of mind had meant the observation seriously. Mergrave, seeming satisfied with the results of his alchemy, handed the glass to the Doctor. 'A mild medicament distilled from herbs, sir, to aid in the further recovery of your wits.'

At the word 'medicament' the hand that was reaching for the glass paused in mid-air. 'You're a Doctor?'

Mergrave acknowledged with a bow of the head. 'A Master of Physic, yes.'

'Not, I suppose, the Doctor,' their visitor enquired, with special emphasis on the word 'the'. 'I've come here to find him . . . I think.'

The three Castrovalvans conferred together, then Ruther turned to the Doctor. 'It must be the Portreeve the Stranger is in search of.' Shardovan seconded this idea. 'The Portreeve, certainly. No one of us else is of the least importance.'

The Doctor remembered the word. 'Portreeve? A sort of Magistrate.'

'A man of the greatest wisdom,' said Shardovan. 'He reads thoroughly the books I merely rearrange.' The Librarian noticed the Doctor's glance towards the neat white bed, and added quickly: 'Yes, you must sleep, sir. You must feast with us another day.' The three gentlemen of Castrovalva made for the door and after cordial goodnights left the Doctor alone.

Or so at first it seemed. The Doctor had not yet tasted the medicine Mergrave had prepared for him, but as he held the glass up to the light and studied it with curiosity, he was startled by a new voice, firm-toned but elderly.

'Drink, my friend. It is a simple concoction of herbs to promote healing sleep.' From behind the arras stepped a bent-backed old man, walking with a stick. Judging by as much of his ruddy complexion as could be seen above his handsome full white beard, he appeared very healthy for his advanced years. 'His father was physician to me, man and boy, and I think I'm testimony enough.'

The Doctor instinctively knew who he was. 'The Portreeve, I presume.'

The old man bowed his head in acknowledgement. 'I see I startled you. Forgive the indirectness of my entrance. I did not wish to advertise my presence to the others. It's past my bedtime, and if they knew I was abroad, they would press me to this feast. For me, as for you, sir, sleep is sometimes better nourishment than good red meat. And, I fear, as rare.'

The Doctor responded to the Portreeve's good-natured laugh, but on being asked his name the Doctor looked puzzled, as if the question contained words beyond his vocabulary. 'I think you do not remember,' the old man concluded, gesturing to the Doctor to drink up. 'No matter, sir. You will very soon find the Doctor.'

'You overheard?'

'No, I've become too deaf of late to listen at doors. The Portreeve smiled, adding: 'I fear my reputation for wisdom will soon be lost. Between ourselves, the gentle people of Castrovalva are too generous with their approbation. I am a man of small talent. I have . . . a device at my disposal. An instrument.'

The Doctor raised an eyebrow. 'Technology? Here?'

'The simplest of devices,' the Portreeve told him. 'When you breakfast with me tomorrow you shall see the source of what my friends are pleased to call my "great wisdom". Now, sleep sir.'

The Doctor was already yawning uncontrollably. He leaned back on the bed, unable to keep his eyes open. 'It has been a long journey. Tell me, Portreeve, off the record . . . Will I find the Doctor here?'

The old man blew out the lantern and silently unlatched the door. 'Oh yes, Doctor. Very soon. Goodnight, Doctor.' The door closed quietly, and the owner of the gentle old voice was gone.

But his final words seemed to remain behind, whispering around the white walls. The Doctor slowly opened his eyes. 'Doctor?' he muttered to himself. But it hurt his head to think, so he shut his eyes again, dismissing the idea.

The moon came and went behind the clouds, teasing them with glimpses of the white walls of Castrovalva above. Tegan stretched down an arm and helped Nyssa clamber up onto the narrow ledge she had barely been able to reach herself, so few were the handholds at this height. The two girls wedged themselves against the cliff wall to rest for a moment and shelter from the biting wind as best they could.

In her state of exhaustion Nyssa was filled with doubts about everything. 'Perhaps we should have told him about Adric,' she said. She meant the Doctor of course; he was constantly in their thoughts.

'Dangerous,' said Tegan. After the long climb the rock behind her back seemed to be reeling drunkenly, trying to tip her into the abyss below. She dug in her heels and braced herself against the imagined motion. When she had got her breath back she said: 'You know the Doctor. He would have dropped everything and gone after him.'

'There might have been a chance. But now . . . Anything might have happened to him . . .' Nyssa tailed off. Something made a rustling sound above them, and then came snaking down, swinging only a few feet from where they were crouched. The moon came out again, and the girls blinked in disbelief.

It was a rope ladder.

When the Portreeve had closed the door softly on the Doctor, he had gone to stand for a while on the flight of steps overlooking the central square. Below him the preparations for the feast were going forward, but he kept to the shadows, preferring to remain unobserved by the bustle of people around the table by the fountain. As he watched, sharing the Castrovalvans' anticipation of the feast, a look of modest, yet almost possessive, pride came over him.

Shardovan and Mergrave were crossing the square immediately below him, and he slipped back behind a column to avoid being seen. Over the chatter and clatter of plates their voices drifted up to him.

'More strangers have arrived, Shardovan . . .' Mergrave was saying. 'They scaled the walls.'

'A new sport to replace hunting?' remarked the Librarian, in his most supercilious voice. 'Who are these Supermen?'

'Not Supermen. You will scarcely believe this, Shardovan. They're . . .' Then the amiable alchemist became quite agitated. 'They're coming . . . They're here. I must tell the Portreeve.'

The two girls entering the square with Ruther caused quite a stir among the Castrovalvan women, who stopped in the middle of their fetching and carrying and began to point and gossip among themselves. Shardovan's mouth fell open, astonished to discover that these were the 'Supermen'.

The strident Australian voice of Tegan topped everything. 'I demand to see the Doctor! We know he's here.'

'We saw him brought in,' Nyssa added rather more politely.

'The Doctor?' echoed Ruther, blinking in his agitation. 'This is most strange. The other visitor told us the same thing.'

Nyssa leaped on the phrase. 'Other visitor?' She turned excitedly to Tegan. 'Of course, they don't know him as the Doctor. He's lost his identity.'

'I demand to see him whoever they think he is,' Tegan repeated. She stared at the Castrovalvan women, who had completely abandoned their tasks and were pressing in around her. 'Get that?'

Ruther glanced across at Shardovan, who nodded his approval. Shooing the gossiping women back to their work, Ruther conducted the girls with the greatest deference towards the steps that led up to the Doctor's quarters. Mergrave was moving to join them, but Shardovan plucked him by the sleeve. 'We will not disturb the Portreeve with this news. Old men need their sleep.'

The Portreeve melted into the inky shadows behind the pillars as Nyssa, Tegan and their Castrovalvan escorts passed him. When they had gone he stepped back into the moonlight and leaned on his stick, looking down at Shardovan.

The Librarian turned, sensing his presence on the terrace behind him. 'Some old men seldom sleep, Shardovan,' said the Portreeve gently. Shardovan raised his eyes to meet the old man's challenge, and for a moment they looked at each other. There was no affection in the gaze, only resentment at the powerful bond between them.

A wedge of light from Mergrave's lantern swept over the neat white bed as the door to the room opened slowly. So profound was his sleep that the Doctor did not stir, and Tegan and Nyssa, hanging back at the door, did not dare wake him.

'Is he all right?' whispered Nyssa.

Mergrave beamed at her. 'Tomorrow his wits will be recovered.'

They stood for a moment, watching the gentle rise and fall of his breathing. 'We'll tell him tomorrow,' Nyssa said.

Tegan wasn't so sure. 'He's still not strong.'

'We must. We have to think of Adric too. I know hardly anything about telebiogenesis. If only there were some books here.'

They went out, drawing the door shut behind them. As it closed, a shadowy figure standing behind it stepped out into the room. On the bed the Doctor stirred, his sleep troubled. The intruder unlatched the door and opened it a fraction to watch the girls retreating down the corridor. A sliver of light fell onto his round young face—a face the girls would have recognised as Adric.

Their climb had exhausted them, and they slept dreamlessly. Nyssa woke next day surprised to find herself completely refreshed, although it was still early. She crept quietly to the window to avoid disturbing Tegan, and looked down into the square.

Below her Castrovalva lay open to the sparkling dawn light, and she could see at once why the textbooks called it the Dwellings of Simplicity. The terraces and steps that led up to the houses all had an inviting neatness about them, like a toy village laid out carefully on a table.

Simple the town might be, but there was nothing drably uniform about it. The buildings surrounding the square were a fascinating mixture of styles, with the eye forever being led into friendly courtyards and alleys, through Roman arches and up the many winding flights of steps.

By the fountain women were clearing away the remains of the feast. Drawn by the fresh morning smell breezing in through the open window, Nyssa could wait no longer. She cast a glance at her companion, decided to leave her to her well-earned sleep, and tiptoed to the door.

She was on her way down the steps when she saw two of the Castrovalvan men disappear behind a colonnade carrying something she thought she recognised. She ran after them, but when she got to the spot it was deserted. Then through the honeysuckle that filligreed the pillars she noticed the two men on one of the higher terraces, and the Zero Cabinet they carried between them was clearly visible.

She ran after them, but she chose the wrong flight of steps. When she eventually caught up with them—the geography of the town was more confusing than she had thought—she called out: 'Wait! That belongs to the Doctor.'

The sun had risen above the roof-tops, and was stealing into the neat white room where the Doctor was still fast asleep when Nyssa opened the door. She beckoned to the two Castrovalvans to follow her, indicated where they should put down the Zero Cabinet, then thanked them quietly and ushered them out.

The Doctor looked so peaceful that she wondered whether to wake him. Then, just as she had decided to let him sleep on, she caught sight of something that almost made her cry out. A big swivel mirror stood beside the dressing table, and in it she saw a dark reflection she knew almost as well as her own.

'Adric!'

'No! Don't turn round.' The boy's voice was husky and urgent. 'I've been waiting for you. Listen, quickly. The Master mustn't find me here.'

Nyssa gasped. 'He's in Castrovalva?'

'He can find me anywhere,' was Adric's grim answer. 'I'm

still in his power. But you mustn't let the Doctor know.'

It was hard not to turn round. Nyssa shook her head. 'We have to tell him.'

Adric was adamant. 'Rescuing me can wait. Please—that's not the most important thing. The Doctor must stay in Castrovalva until his regeneration is complete.'

'Wait here!' said Nyssa. 'I must get Tegan.'

'No! Don't tell anybody you saw me. Nobody, you understand.'

The compulsion to turn round was too strong for her. In the flesh the boy looked even paler than his reflection, and there was an odd light in his eyes. She ran to him, but as she drew close he reeled back. A scattering of brilliant yellow sparks blinded her as she touched him, and when she opened her eyes again he was gone.

In the bed the Doctor stirred. Nyssa went to him, not knowing whether to tell him or keep her promise to Adric—if it was Adric she had seen. The Doctor stretched luxuriously and opened his eyes.

'Nyssa!' he said, recognising her immediately. 'Lovely morning.'

It was true; the white room was full of sunlight now. 'Are you all right, Doctor?' Nyssa asked in a small voice.

'Better than just all right,' he replied with a grin as he sat up in bed. 'I'm practically my old self again. Or rather—my new self!'

Nyssa said she was very happy to hear it, and the Doctor didn't doubt she was. But underneath he sensed her unease; something was troubling her. But she was always a very independent person, and no doubt she would tell him about it in her own good time.

The cruel steel wires of the web trembled under the motion of the struggling boy they held transfixed, but their grip was unyielding. With a whirring sound the elevating device brought the Master's piercing black eyes into level confrontation with Adric's.

'No, I won't do it. I won't . . .' the boy cried, shaking his head like someone caught up in a nightmare.

'But you have done it,' came the drip of that honey-and-vinegar voice. 'A perfect impersonation of yourself. Now we will remain untroubled by the Doctor's meddling while our plans mature.'

9

The Occlusion Closes In

The Portreeve's chamber was a tall, stately room, with half-timbered walls plastered in white. The Doctor pushed back his chair after the most satisfying breakfast he could remember for a long time, and let his eye run along the intriguing oak beams supporting the roof. High up in one wall a gallery overlooked the room—rather curiously placed, the Doctor thought, for it was set directly above a huge fireplace with oversized fire-irons to match. The opposite wall was dominated by an enormous tapestry that portrayed a hunting scene in subtle greens and blues. Like many of the other objects he had noticed about him elsewhere in Castrovalva, the furnishings and fittings of the Portreeve's chamber were meticulously crafted. He congratulated the Portreeve on the care and attention that had gone into their making.

'Time is at the root of it all,' the old man observed, gracefully brushing away the compliment. 'We do so little on Castrovalva, sir, and therefore what we do, we have time to do well.'

Women appeared, and began to clear away the remnants of the meal.

'I like your Castrovalva, Portreeve,' the Doctor said. He indicated Tegan and Nyssa, who, hungry after their long climb, were still busy demolishing the breakfast. 'Clever of them to have brought me here.'

The Portreeve smiled. 'I fear we must be a little dull after the habitual excitements you describe.'

During the meal the Doctor had told him something of his adventures with the Daleks, the Ogrons and his other many adversaries. The conversation had heartened Nyssa and Tegan, for it was clear that the Doctor's memory had returned almost completely, although he still seemed very hazy about the journey to Castrovalva. Adric had not been mentioned once, and the girls had agreed they would leave that ugly question until they were sure the Doctor was completely recovered.

Nyssa saw a pale, introverted face peering in at the window, and recognised the man she had heard addressed as Shardovan. A moment later the door onto the terrace opened with a creak, and the tall figure was silhouetted against the sunlight.

'The volumes you asked for, Portreeve,' the newcomer said drily. He stepped into the room, making way for a woman carrying a pile of books.

The Portreeve rose to greet him. 'Thank you, Shardovan. I have finished with those.' He waved a hand towards a table strewn with open volumes. The Castrovalvan women put down the books and began to collect up the others.

Tegan could no longer restrain a question that had been troubling her. 'The only thing I can't make out—if this place is so ideal how come the women do all the work around here?'

She had directed the question towards Shardovan, as if in some way she thought he was personally to blame. He raised an eyebrow. 'There is an alternative arrangement?'

'On Tegan's planet they're trying out an idea called equality.' This remark of the Doctor's was perfectly even-handed, but Tegan took it as a declaration of the Doctor's support, and continued aggressively: 'Isn't it fairer if everybody's treated the same?'

'I confess,' Shardovan declared loftily, 'that I have never thought upon the subject.'

'Then perhaps you ought to?' Tegan snapped, and received an admonishing look from the Doctor that suggested she was pushing the rules of hospitality too far.

It was the Portreeve's diplomatic intervention that cooled things down. 'In Castrovalva we pursue our lives as best we may, not as best we could.' As ever he spoke lightly, but in a voice that made you listen for wisdom in his meaning. 'We lack reformers. Stay with us and improve our minds. Perhaps I should introduce you officially . . . Tegan and Nyssa . . .

Shardovan, our Librarian.'

'A library!' Nyssa exchanged a glance with Tegan, and the thought passed between them that they might be able to research into telebiogenesis. Shardovan bowed and said he would be glad if they cared to visit it.

The Portreeve had promised to show the Doctor the 'device' from which he drew his reputation for wisdom, so the two men were happy to let Nyssa and Tegan go off with Shardovan for an hour or so. The Portreeve saw them out and closed the door. He returned to find the Doctor admiring the great hanging tapestry.

'Whoever made this certainly had a way with needle and thread, Portreeve.' The other nodded his agreement and stood for a moment musing in front of it. The Doctor was not particularly impatient to move on, but he thought it polite to remind the Portreeve of the 'device'.

The Portreeve was amused. 'It stands before you, Doctor!' He gestured with his stick across the expanse of woven green and blue thread. 'I have returned the picture to its state of yesterday, by way of demonstration. Look, Doctor—we can relive your journey.'

And with these words the Portreeve drew him close to the tapestry and pointed to part of it the Doctor had not noticed before, where the coloured threads depicted Nyssa and Tegan carrying the Zero Cabinet across the stream. And the picture moved.

For a long time the Doctor paced about the room, regarding the astonishing tapestry from various angles, sometimes stepping up close to inspect the texture, and at other times walking back to the opposite wall to take in the whole panorama. As he watched, the tapestry unfolded the story of his arrival at Castrovalva, not with constant motion like the moving image on the TARDIS viewer screen, but in a series of delicately detailed tableaux, each dissolving almost imperceptibly into the next.

'I've seen many extraordinary things, Portreeve, in the course of a long life. But this—it's extra-extraordinary. How often do these pictures renew themselves?'

'Oh, by no means all the time,' said the Portreeve, his pride in the device giving way to a modest desire to apologise for its too flamboyant virtuosity. 'Life here in the main is slow and unremarkable. Only an occasion like your visit disturbs the cycles enough to register on the tapestry.'

The Doctor had discovered a magnifying glass lying on the table and used it to peer closely at the threads. 'Some form of fast-particle projection, I suppose?'

The Portreeve seemed faintly embarrassed by the question. He brushed some speck from the tapestry, producing a small cloud of dust. 'Our forebears had many skills, now forgotten.'

'But if—as I understand from your Librarian and his friends —they were savages . . .?'

He moved to take a look behind the tapestry, but stopped at a glance from the Portreeve, who said: 'There is no doubt some complexity behind it. From what you tell me, you had better avoid such things until you are restored.'

The Doctor had to agree that the Portreeve was probably right, but in spite of the suggestion of giddiness he felt when close to the tapestry he returned a moment later for another close look at the finely wrought detail. Now Nyssa and Tegan were carrying the Zero Cabinet through the thick of the wood. 'You know,' said the Doctor, 'I had no idea I was putting them to so much trouble. It's a very long way for three young people to carry me.'

'Three, Doctor?'

'Yes . . . Tegan, Nyssa and . . . and . . . Tegan . . .' The Doctor paused in confusion, and began again, counting on his fingers. 'Tegan, Nyssa and Tegan. No, no, silly of me. Nyssa, Tegan and Nyssa.' He turned back to the tapestry for adjudication. 'Nyssa . . . Tegan . . .'

He looked at the three fingers he was holding up, which seemed right, and then at the picture on the tapestry—which also seemed right. But if you took away one finger for each of the characters portrayed in the tapestry you were left with one finger too many, no matter how many times you did it. At last his reeling mind stumbled on a conclusion from all this complex calculation. 'D'you know, Portreeve, I'm sure there's someone missing.'

The Portreeve apologised for the tapestry; it was interfering with his recuperation. A walk in the sunshine would soon restore his wits. With a gesture towards the piles of books Shardovan had brought him, the Portreeve excused himself from accompanying him further than the door, so the Doctor was soon wandering alone in the village square.

A crowd of women were gathered around a trough that had replaced the banqueting table beside the fountain, and there was much carrying to and fro of wet washing. As the Doctor walked past them they turned and giggled behind their hands, amused at the serious way he was nodding to himself and counting over and over again on his fingers. He waved back to them absent-mindedly, and resumed his intense calculations.

'One . . . two . . .' He lowered himself onto the bench by the fountain and tried again. 'One . . . two . . . No, no, no . . . One . . . two . . .'

A small child interrupted its playing with a pile of stones and came to stand beside the Doctor, staring in fascination at the grown-up's inability to put two and two together.

'One!' said the Doctor firmly to himself, intending to put up with no more of this nonsense from a mere string of cardinal numbers. 'Two! Er . . .'

'Three, sir,' said the small child.

The Doctor bent forward to look into the little round face. 'What?'

'Three, sir, is what comes after two,' said the child seriously.

'That's exactly what I thought,' said the Doctor.

'And then four and then five and then six and then seven . . .'

The Doctor put his hands to his ears. 'Stop! You've making me dizzy.' And then, afraid that he might have offended the child, added: 'Well done. We must give you a badge for mathematical excellence.'

The phrase had hardly passed his lips when he struck his forehead and jumped up so suddenly that the frightened child scurried away to the reassuring skirt of its mother by the washing trough.

'Adric!' the Doctor exclaimed, and set off across the square at a very un-Castrovalvan pace.

The visit to the library had not after all produced any information about telebiogenesis, in fact the Technical Section was farcically small. It was a gloomy building with tall narrow windows, as if the shelves upon shelves of books that lined the walls were squeezing out the light. No wonder Shardovan was so pale if he spent all day in the dark alleys between the bookcases.

The main strength of the library, as Shardovan loftily pointed out, lay with the Humanities: Arts and Crafts, Languages, and a great deal of History. They came across a whole row of ancient dusty tomes entitled *A Condensed Chronicle of Castrovalva*; these certainly weren't going to help them much with Adric. But Shardovan, whom they kept glimpsing through the bookcases as they moved from section to section, suddenly reappeared beside them with unctuous recommendations of other books on other shelves, and this obvious diversion aroused their curiosity.

Tegan was determined to assert herself. 'No, these will do nicely, thank you very much. I know the Doctor will be interested.' After an icy exchange of views in which Nyssa had to intervene, they took away as many volumes of the *Chronicle* as they could carry, and emerged blinking into the sunlight.

'Well, as long as we're here we might as well learn something about Castrovalvan history,' said Tegan, reassuring herself with the sound of her own voice—for some reason they had been whispering in the library. She was conscious of Shardovan watching them from the doorway, a long white face in the shadows.

They hauled the books back to the Doctor's room and leafed through them while they waited for him to come back from the Portreeve. But when he threw open the door he was clearly not in the mood for reading.

'Where is he? Where's Adric?'

The two girls looked at each other. 'You told him!' said Tegan accusingly.

'Of course not,' said Nyssa, uncharacteristically flustered. 'Adric told me not to.'

'Adric told you?' snapped the Doctor. This threw Nyssa into even more confusion, and she began to apologise for her stupidity. 'Never mind the excuses. I think it's time I heard all about this.'

So they told him everything, and much to Tegan's astonishment Nyssa added her own confession about the visitation from Adric. The Doctor listened with an intense concentration that his constant pacing of the room and occasional glances out of the window couldn't disguise. And then he made the decision they had predicted.

'Come on, the TARDIS.'

Before they had time to argue he had thrown open the door and was hurrying along the terrace. The two girls ran after him, but as they descended the steps Nyssa realised they had forgotten something very important, and called out: 'Doctor! The Zero Cabinet.'

The Doctor brushed aside the suggestion. 'We can't go through all that again.'

'But once we get outside the walls . . .' said Tegan. He seemed to have forgotten that Castrovalva was giving him protection.

'We'll have to hope, won't we?' was the Doctor's not very constructive reply. By this time they had arrived at the square. The Doctor ran up to the group of women washing clothes in the trough. 'What's the quickest way out of here?'

The women looked the Doctor up and down. Then in answer to his question they all pointed in different directions.

'I see,' said the Doctor. 'Well, that's democracy for you.' He picked the most likely exit route, called over his shoulder to Tegan and Nyssa to follow, and together they headed for a flight of steps that descended from the square.

The steps led through an archway in a wall flecked with crimson ivy, and then down to more steps. 'I don't think we came in this way,' said Nyssa. The Doctor brushed away her doubts at first, but when the steps levelled out onto a covered walk and they looked over the parapet down upon the roofs of yet more houses—a sort of second Castrovalva set at the foot of the one they knew—he paused for a moment to mop his brow.

'I always did have a terrible sense of direction. Still, as long as we keep going down . . .' There were more steps at the end of the walk, and they began to descend again.

Tegan suddenly stopped and leaned over the balustrade. 'It's impossible!' Nyssa saw it too, and tugged at the Doctor's sleeve. Below them, exactly as they had left it, was the village square.

The women were still getting on with their washing. The Doctor and his two companions arrived at the fountain to find Mergrave and Ruther waiting for them. The physician was looking less than his usual cheerful self. 'Leaving us, Doctor, we hear?' Mergrave said.

Ruther was positively agitated. 'I beg you, Doctor. Reconsider this too hasty departure.'

'For reasons of health if not of courtesy,' added Mergrave.

But the Doctor would not allow himself to be detained. 'Sorry, it's too important. Mush dash now . . . come back later. Where do those steps take us?'

'Out, sir, if you insist,' replied Ruther. The Doctor thanked the two Castrovalvans and set off at an even faster pace.

At the bottom of the steps was a covered colonnade dripping with honeysuckle which Nyssa recognised as the place where she had spotted the Zero Cabinet on her early morning walk, although she seemed to remember it as overlooking the square. They ran to the portico at the end and found yet another flight of steps. These led less steeply downwards under a vault of trees, and took them eventually to a small gazebo overlooking the spot they had started from.

'That wreched square again,' exclaimed Tegan. 'What's happening, Doctor?'

The Doctor halted to survey the array of roofs and parapets. 'Ssh, concentrate. This could be very serious.' The perspective of receding terraces certainly gave an illusion of distance to the lower slopes that terminated in the white perimeter walls. But the picture was deceptive—the Doctor knew that now. If you looked carefully you became aware that there was a second perspective at work that brought the distant outskirts closer and set them above the town.

From this angle Castrovalva seemed normal enough to Tegan, if a bit larger than she remembered it. But Nyssa saw what was happening. 'It's as if space had been folded in on itself.'

'Very likely!' said the Doctor tersely, and immediately set off again, this time leading them back the way they had come. 'Quick!' he called out, 'there may still be time to reverse the sense.'

Tegan and Nyssa scrambled after the nimble white figure of the Doctor. He seemed fit enough to bound up the steps four at a time, but there was evidence of his returning confusion in the moments when he stopped at vantage points to take stock of the surroundings.

Nyssa's first thought had been that climbing too fast to the lofty hamlet of Castrovalva without taking time for proper acclimatisation had produced in the Doctor the classic symptoms of high-altitude oedema, a sort of water on the brain. But the evidence of the landscape was irrefutable: the confusion was outside, part of Castrovalva itself. Soon, Nyssa guessed, it would even start to affect their own judgement.

The worst moment came when the steps they were ascending turned a corner, and they found the way blocked by a tall, thin figure standing in an archway. The Doctor seemed to weaken suddenly, and the two girls rushed to stop him falling.

'What is the occasion of this haste?' asked Shardovan in his quiet, hollow voice. The two girls instinctively backed away, half-carrying the Doctor down the steps again until they came to an alternative route that led them out of range of the dark gaze of the Librarian. The path continued downwards, and they knew it would carry them back to the inevitable square.

They paused for breath in a small arbour. The Doctor leaned against one of the pillars, visibly weaker now. He seemed to be gasping to tell them something.

'It's affecting him,' Nyssa explained to Tegan. 'Some very complex spatial disturbance. We've got to get him back to the Zero Cabinet immediately.' She went to the edge of the balcony to decide their next step.

Tegan leaned close against the pillar to hear what the Doctor was saying. 'Castrovalva . . .' The voice came faintly. 'Folding in . . . deliberately.' And then Nyssa was signalling to them, and they were moving again. More steps, another terrace, and then they were at a door that Tegan recognised.

'Quick, get him inside,' said Nyssa.

It was the Doctor's room! The girls helped the Doctor in and looked around for the Zero Cabinet. There was no sign of it anywhere.

They tried to lead him towards the bed, but he shook them off and stumbled to the window. A strange noise escaped his lips and they ran to his side. Painfully he found his voice. 'Recursive Occlusion! Someone's manipulating Castrovalva. We're caught in a space/time trap!'

Tegan and Nyssa looked out of the window, gazing in wonder and fear at what they saw. Below them and above them the whole of Castrovalva, square, walks, archways, colonnades, steps, porticos, gazebos and balustrades, appeared as a jigsaw puzzle of pieces jammed together by a blind man with no regard for sense or shape.

But it was the Castrovalvan population that unintentionally brought the final touch of horror to the scene. The washing women by the fountain, the collection of gossipping old men outside the library, and Ruther and Mergrave crossing the square together deep in conversation—each seemed heedless of the illogical geography, and moved in their separate and various dimensions, up, down, sideways and upside-down like dolls in a doll's house seen through a kaleidoscope.

10

The Clue of the *Chronicle*

The mind-numbing scene outside the window made Tegan close her eyes and clutch the window-sill. Nyssa had to look away too, and she saw the Doctor stagger back, about to fall. Her cry made Tegan forget her own sick feeling, and the two girls rushed to catch hold of him. But he brusquely disengaged himself from their support.

'No time for that. We've got to find out what's causing this Occlusion before the real damage starts. Follow me.' He moved towards the door confidently enough, but before he was half-way across the room his legs buckled under him and Tegan had to run forward and catch him. 'Please . . .' he said in a voice that was suddenly small, 'find the Zero Cabinet.'

Nyssa didn't hesitate. 'The Portreeve! He'll help us. Wait here, Doctor.'

The Doctor caught her arm. 'The Occlusion . . . it won't be dangerous to you at this stage. But be careful. It's going to get harder and harder to find your way about.' Tegan was still holding onto him determinedly, and showed every sign of being about to fuss over him, so he added: 'Better take the air-hostess person with you.'

They weren't at all happy about leaving him alone, but he became agitated in his insistence. The two girls rushed out, realising that there wasn't time to argue. The sooner they found the Zero Cabinet the sooner they could get the Doctor back into it.

The largest piece of furniture in the room was the looking-glass; full length and double width, its mahogany frame swivelled in a U-shaped cradle of the same deep dark wood, making it altogether a very handsome addition to the room. At this moment the Doctor was oblivious to its finer points, but did rely heavily on its old-fashioned virtue of solidity, for as soon as the two girls had gone another wave of vertigo overcame him, and he had to grab at its knobs for support. Nausea flooded over him, shaking loose old memories of other Occlusions, and he grappled among this flotsam, trying to remember something useful, some How or Why that would give him a small say in his own fate.

Waves. Propagation Theory. Speed of light. He concentrated on light, and could only think of light-coloured, lightweight cricketing outfits, millions of them, reflected and re-reflected down an eternal corridor of mirrors.

Mirrors! Yes, that was it. The Doctor forced his gaze in the direction of the big looking-glass, an idea forming in his head. Then, with a massive effort of will, he began to drag it towards the window.

Nyssa and Tegan quickly discovered that the Doctor was right: it had become even harder to find your way around. Once outside, the really misleading thing was that the fragmentation of the geography they had seen from the Doctor's window was no longer obvious, in fact there was nothing you could point to and say 'That looks wrong'. At last they accidentally stumbled upon the town square, and there they came across Ruther, who seemed completely unaware of the terrible tangle his Castrovalva had become.

The only difficulty he could see was in their plan to talk to the Portreeve. 'I think we should prepare ourselves for disappointment,' he said as he preceded them down the steps. 'It is unusual for the Portreeve to grant two audiences on the same day.'

'Just take us to him,' Tegan insisted. 'We'll cross that bridge when we come to it.'

They crossed a great many bridges, but they did not come to it. In the most amiable possible way their guide led them round in circles. 'Look at that!' Tegan exclaimed, when after a long walk the winding path took them out onto a small balcony, and the ubiquitous town square lay insolently below them again. Evidently the Castrovalvans were proud of the view from here, because someone had mounted a swivelling brass telescope on the balustrade.

Ruther obligingly hooked a pair of steel-rimmed spectacles over his ears. 'Yes, that is the square,' he agreed.

'But we keep coming back to it,' Nyssa said.

'Naturally,' said Ruther.

Tegan became quite heated. 'But you must see there's something going wrong here.'

With the air of one arguing a case that is really quite simple, although it may sound complicated, Ruther explained carefully: 'There are, as you have observed, steps that rise from the square, and others that lead downwards from it, while other walks debouch laterally. An equitable arrangement, surely, allowing for much variety of movement.'

'You're not going to tell me you don't realise . . .' Tegan began, but was stopped by a warning shake of the head from Nyssa.

'I do not imply,' Ruther went on, oblivious of all this, 'that improvements might not be made. I have myself suggested that an ornamental lake should complete the view.' He pushed his spectacles onto his forehead and stooped to put his eye to the telescope. 'Nevertheless, you will find the vista exemplary from here.'

While he made delicate adjustments to the brass knobs, Tegan took the opportunity to whisper to Nyssa: 'But they must know. They're all in this together.'

'I think they are all in it together,' said Nyssa. 'And that's exactly why they don't know. Don't you see? If they're part of the recursion themselves, they'll be the last to know . . .' She broke off, looking over the balustrade in the direction that Ruther was pointing the telescope. He lifted his eye from the eyepiece and noticing her interest handed over the instrument.

Tegan thought her friend was training the telescope on the tall, thin figure of Shardovan, who happened to be crossing the square at that moment. But she was wrong: the object that had caught Nyssa's eye, and which was now captured in the magnified circle of light at the end of the brass tube, was, as she saw for herself when Nyssa urgently beckoned her over . . . the washing trough.

In the foreshortened perspective the trough at first looked unfamiliar. But then, as the women walked away from it, carrying the last of their wet bundles, it was easy to see what had attracted Nyssa's attention. Tegan chided herself for not noticing it before. The receptacle the women had been using for their laundry was nothing more nor less than the Zero Cabinet.

It had taken all the Doctor's strength to drag the mirror in front of the window, and now he leant weakly against it while he caught his breath. With an atomic weight of around 108 the thin film of silver on the back of the glass was not the heaviest of elements, but it had a usefully high conductivity. He was hoping it would go some way towards deflecting whatever it was out there that was sapping his strength, and give him a little breathing space to think out his next move.

There is an official Time-Lord strategy you are taught even as a small child: in circumstances of near-defeat you take stock of the forces that are working on your behalf, your assets, and then separately assess the forces working against you, your liabilities. This leads directly to the next stage: devising a logical plan that will increase the former and diminish the latter. The dictum had always struck the Doctor as typically Gallifreyan—that is to say arid, abstract and artificial. The only really stimulating thing about defeat, death and disaster is that all the rule-books go out of the window, and you are permitted to improvise under the purest inspiration of all—blind panic.

But for the present his numbed brain allowed neither panic nor inspiration, and he was grateful to have the tired old Gallifreyan formula to fall back on. He enumerated his liabilities. One: something, amorphous and insidiously destructive, had invaded Castrovalva. Two: he himself was especially vulnerable to whatever it was because of the unfortunate timing of the process of regeneration. And three (and by no means least): at this very time when he had too little strength even to save himself, his young friend Adric was in desperate need of his help.

So much for the liabilities. His assets were . . . well, what, precisely? Two intelligent young helpers (but his responsibility for them make them equally liabilities) . . . and a still serviceable cricketing outfit.

This was really a feebly short list to put on the positive side of the equation. He cast his eye around the room to see what else he could commandeer as an ally, and it lighted on the volumes of the *Condensed Chronicle of Castrovalva* the girls had left behind them.

The mirror did seem to be offering some protection, and for the moment the Doctor was able to let go of it and take a few tentative steps across to the table. In the nearly eight hundred years of his being, much of that time spent in travel, the Doctor had arrived at the working hypothesis that experience is no substitute for books. He had a healthy respect for anything his fellow creatures felt was worth committing to print, although the profuseness of their publications often made him wish that reading could be got through more quickly and writing made less easy, perhaps with a universal rule that all books be hand-carved in granite with a pin.

But reading was never the first thing the Doctor did with a new book. He picked one up and flicked idly through it, then held the flyleaf up to the light to inspect it for a watermark. Then he opened two of the other books, sniffed one of them carefully and glanced at its table of contents.

'Must be about five hundred years old . . .' he said aloud. He was about to put it down (it being volume one, and you never start to read a multi-volumed work at volume one) when a piece of paper slipped from between its leaves. He smoothed it out on the table and saw that it was closely covered with fine handwriting. 'Hello . . .' he muttered, 'that's very odd indeed.'

The Doctor heard a second voice in the room, something between a tuneless humming and a discreet cough, and glanced up to find a chubby balding head peeking round the door.

'Mergrave!' exclaimed the Doctor. 'Just the chap.'

The amiable physician had come to see if there was any more call for his herbal remedy. The Doctor said he was feeling much better now—which was an exaggeration—and attributed it all to his friend's medical skills, making no mention of the mirror. There was a motive behind this praise: the Doctor wanted

Mergrave to run an errand for him.

While he was away, the Doctor poured over the books, referring constantly to the piece of paper he had found. Eventually Mergrave returned with a trio of muscular Castrovalvan girls, each of whom carried a pile of dusty leather-bound volumes. It was the rest of the *Condensed Chronicle*.

The Doctor looked up from his studies. 'Well done, Mergrave.' The physician put down the small flask he was carrying and shooed the girls away. 'And many thanks,' the Doctor went on, inspecting the new additions to his collection. 'I'm very fond of History, and now I seem to have time on my hands.' He had a way of gently easing the covers back and peering down into the hollow spine of the bindings, as if the History he sought resided there rather than the pages.

Mergrave had noticed the mirror blocking the window, and perhaps with the idea of giving the Doctor more light for his labours was on the point of moving it back to its original place. 'No please!' said the Doctor quickly. 'Small remedy of my own—more of a whim really. Helps to keep it out.'

Mergrave appeared amused. 'It? And what, sir, is it?'

The Doctor gestured towards the books, which were now lying higgledy-piggledy all over the table. 'That's precisely what I'm trying to find out. Tell me, Mergrave . . . What do you see out of the window?'

Mergrave humoured him good-naturedly by peering round the mirror.

'The town square, the library, the Portreeve's house. And my own Pharmacy. In fine, sir, the Dwellings of Castrovalva.'

The next question was crucial, but the Doctor asked it casually. 'And it all . . . makes sense to you?'

Mergrave laughed warmly at this. 'A strange question. I see, sir, you are another Shardovan.' He poured some drops of liquid from the flask into a glass.

'Shardovan?' interposed the Doctor.

'A metaphysician like yourself, sir.'

'Has he ever asked you the same question?'

'On several occasions, during his more melancholy moods.' Mergrave handed the glass to the Doctor. 'He too can be a little fevered in his imaginings.'

The Doctor paused with the glass at his lips. 'How do I know you're telling the truth?'

The physician's face froze into an expression of great dignity. 'Because, sir, I maintain I am. And I am a man of my word.'

The Time Lord fixed him with a level gaze. 'That's a perfect example of recursion,' the Doctor said eventually. 'And recursion, Mergrave, is what we're up against.' He fumbled in his pocket and produced a stick of chalk. Indicating the back of the mirror, where the expanse of dark wood was unfinished and rough enough to serve as a blackboard, he said: 'Draw me a map. The town plan of Castrovalva.'

The amiable chemist went to work. The Doctor stood beside him, the glass of herbal preparation neglected in his hand.

Mergrave dusted the chalk from his fingers and stepped back to survey his handiwork. 'The library . . . the Square . . . the Portreeve's house . . . Mmmm . . .' said the Doctor. 'Where's your pharmacy?' Mergrave indicated a modest rectangle towards the right-hand corner, and the Doctor nodded. But then the physician went on: '. . . and here, and here, and here also.' His stubby finger tapped three other locations on the map.

The Doctor's eyebrow lifted. 'Four pharmacies, in a little place like this?'

Mergrave sounded surprised. 'No sir. I have but one.'

'You've drawn it four times,' the Doctor felt bound to point out.

'It may be approached, sir, by many different routes.' Mergrave appeared quite baffled at the Doctor's inability to grasp the obvious.

The Doctor looked hard into Mergrave's eyes. Then he raised the glass in his hand and sipped it slowly with every sign of satisfaction. '*Valeriana officinalis* . . .' he pronounced, '*Santicula europaea* . . . and just a hint of rosemary.'

'I see you understand medicine, Doctor!'

'Not as well as you do,' said the Doctor, setting down the empty glass. 'But I'm afraid that one of us is a little deluded about Geography.' He borrowed back the chalk from Mergrave. 'I wonder if your mind would be open to a slightly different way of looking at it?' And carefully avoiding words longer than four syllables, the Doctor took Mergrave through a

94

simplified version of Euclidian topology . . .

Out in the square the Zero Cabinet was being emptied into the fountain. 'You hid this deliberately.' Tegan's loud Australian voice drew nervous giggles from the Castrovalvan women, but her anger was directed at Shardovan.

'Assuredly, ma'am, no impropriety was intended,' came the dignified reply.

Tegan turned on the women, hating them for their readiness to play the role of a silly female chorus. 'You're all part of this. It's a conspiracy.' At last Nyssa managed to calm her down, while Ruther explained to the Castrovalvan women, and to Shardovan, that the visitors were temporarily suffering from the delusion that their friend the Doctor had been ensnared. By this time Tegan didn't trust anybody, and insisted that she and Nyssa and no one else should carry the Zero Cabinet back to the Doctor. Ruther followed at a respectful distance, but ran around in front of them when they reached the Doctor's door to rap smartly on it with his knuckles.

'Yes, yes . . . come in,' said a scratchy, irritated voice from inside. They found a very distracted Mergrave staring at the chalk map which the Doctor had richly annotated with numbers in an effort to explain his own world-view. In the process they had exhausted each other, and despite the combined benefits of the mirror and the valerian the Doctor was looking particularly weak.

'We've found it!' Tegan announced, as she and Nyssa dragged in the Zero Cabinet. 'And no thanks to these Castrovalvan people. He kept leading us round and round and back to the square.'

'That's Castrovalva, not Ruther,' said the Doctor, certain now of at least that much. He turned to Ruther. 'I suppose you know where the Portreeve lives?'

'Nothing is more sure, sir.'

'Well put.' The Doctor handed over the piece of chalk. 'Show us on the map.' Ruther put on his spectacles and studied the back of the mirror carefully before speaking. Then he made small chalk marks on the mahogany. 'This is the Portreeve's house, sir . . . And this . . . and this . . . and this.'

The Doctor turned silently to the girls, inviting them to take in the implications of this demonstration. Mergrave, whose neat dark suit had somehow become covered in chalk dust, joined Ruther by the map and, clasping his hands together to contain the slight tremble that had developed in them, said: 'The Doctor has been explaining to me . . . I almost grasp it . . .' But it was hard to tell whether he was merely eager to be polite.

'There is something amiss with the map?' Ruther asked.

'There's something amiss with Castrovalva,' said the Doctor. 'But because your perception system is part of it, you just don't see it.'

Ruther nodded diplomatically, willing to humour all parties. 'I am a rational man, sir. Explain this interesting idea.'

The Doctor found it painful to pull together his thoughts on the subject for a second time. If his diagnosis was correct the Castrovalvans were suffering from some form of post-hypnotic mass suggestion. Having just gone through something similar himself, the Doctor was reminded of the famous experiment where the subject is persuaded that there is no such thing as the number ten, and is then asked to count his fingers.

He began again with Ruther as he had with Mergrave, using the map to confront him with the contradictions inherent in the delusion. But the strain of concentration was beginning to tell on the Doctor, and after a minute or two of tangled explanation Nyssa urged him to get back into the Zero Cabinet.

'Yes, yes . . . in a minute,' he said, and then became angry because he had completely lost his thread. A question he had been meaning to ask for his own clarification popped into his head. 'Tell me, Ruther—or Mergrave . . . If this is the "condensed" history, where is the full version?'

The two Castrovalvans were amused by the question. 'The volumes before you contain a condensation of the actual history itself,' said Mergrave, and Ruther added: 'What you are pleased to call the full version has taken our ancestors centuries to live through. However fond you may be of reading, sir, you would not want to spend that long with a book.'

The Doctor made no immediate reply to this unusual turn in the conversation. Instead he picked up one of the books and weighed it in his hand. 'This volume chronicles the rise of

Castrovalva out of an alliance of warring hunters twelve hundred years ago. Or purports to chronicle . . .'

Ruther, who had been patient through the Doctor's increasingly confused explanation, began to show a trace of irritation. 'Purports, you say? That, sir, is our official History.'

'From Castrovalva's first beginnings to the present day,' Mergrave added.

'I'm no expert on books,' said the Doctor untruthfully, 'but I have the strongest possible hunch that these are forgeries.'

Ruther gave up trying to conceal his indignation. 'What do you say, sir!'

'Oh, the paper, threads and binding are as near the real thing as maybe. But the contents are faked.' The Doctor was showing the strain, and probably didn't realise the obvious offence he was giving to the two Castrovalvans. Nyssa intervened, suggesting that he should at least explain what had brought him to this conclusion. He tried to respond to the suggestion, but found it hard to concentrate on the line of argument. 'There is a . . . There's something we're all overlooking.'

He staggered and had to be helped to the bed by Nyssa. 'Yes? What, Doctor.'

'Not sure . . . I'm overlooking it too. But I'm certain the whole history's been invented.'

'By Shardovan?' asked Tegan, who had been leafing through one of the books trying to work out what on earth the Doctor was on about.

The Doctor looked up at Mergrave and Ruther, as if he expected them to provide an answer. Ruther had regained his composure and simply returned his gaze with politeness touched by a hint of frost, while beside him the physician shook his head and tut-tutted over this new deterioration of the Doctor's mind.

'Why would anyone want to do that, Doctor?' Nyssa persisted. 'To hide something? Something about the real history?'

The Doctor's next utterance floated up from the wreckage of his sinking consciousness as he leant back to rest. It came as a whisper, but the occupants of the room all heard it, and the profound question it implied hung in their silence long after the Doctor had closed his eyes. 'If there ever was a real history,' he said.

11

The World through the Eyes of Shardovan

Outside on the terrace a convocation of Castrovalvan women, hearing that their unfortunate visitor had lost his wits, had gathered to pool their condolences and their curiosity. The sudden opening of the door caused a flurry of interest, and they pressed forward to see into the room, making it difficult for Mergrave to push his way out through the gathering.

'The visitor is weaker, but receiving our best attentions,' he announced in answer to their persistent questioning. 'Now let me pass.' He had an urgent message for the Portreeve, so they parted respectfully to let him go by.

The Castrovalvan women missed the chance to catch sight of the Doctor. He was already in the Zero Cabinet when Mergrave opened the door, and it was not until it closed again that the Doctor's hand emerged from the Cabinet, craned around like a swan looking for its cygnets, then beckoned across the room.

The object of the hand's attention was Ruther, who crossed the room with good enough grace and positioned himself awkwardly on the floor beside the Doctor. The girls had partially drawn the lid over the Cabinet, and it would have been more comfortable for Ruther to sit on it, but somehow that did not seem decent. The swan-neck hand had disappeared back under cover, returning almost immediately with a piece of paper.

Ruther recognised the handwriting immediately. 'This is Shardovan's hand. The Librarian.'

'Shardovan . . .' came the meditative whisper from inside the cabinet. 'I thought as much . . .'

Ruther adjusted his spectacles and began to peruse the manuscript. But the convoluted prose was so entangled with abstruse metaphysical observations, profusely cross-referenced against the pages and volumes of the *Condensed Chronicle*, that he was not inclined to read on. In any case the swan-neck hand was somewhat peremptorily flicking its fingers for the return of the paper. Ruther handed it back, and there being no further activity from inside the Cabinet, returned to his study of the chalk map, where the two young women continued their unconvincing geography lesson.

In due course the door opened again and Mergrave hurried back into the room to the accompaniment of a chorus of questions from the women outside. He poured a glass from the refilled flask he had brought back with him, and carried it to the Doctor's side. 'The Portreeve is happy to see you,' he whispered to the pale face framed in the rectangle that remained above the partially replaced lid. 'I wonder, however, since you are not strong, how you will be travelling . . .?'

'We're going to carry him there,' said Tegan. 'He'll be all right as long as he stays in the cabinet.'

The Doctor's arm journeyed out towards the glass that Mergrave was proffering, and he tilted his head up to sip some of its contents. But his hand was shaking, and the glass slipped from his fingers and broke on the floor.

Tegan ran forward officiously. 'I'm sorry. Would you mind waiting outside?' Her eyes included Ruther in the invitation.

While Tegan was receiving their polite expressions of sympathy with an air-hostess smile, and ushering them out to join the murmuring women on the terrace outside, Nyssa bent to pick up the broken glass. She heard a whisper from inside the cabinet and lowered her head to listen.

'One little suggestion . . .' said the Doctor. His voice was barely audible, and she may have imagined that its tone carried the faintest hint of impishness. She had to lean right into the Cabinet to hear what he whispered next.

Tegan was surprised, annoyed and flattered, all at the same time, by the interest the Castrovalvan women showed in the Doctor's condition: Was his madness confirmed? Was it contagious? Was he dead yet? Mergrave and Ruther helped quiet the clamour of questions, and with the threat of sending them away altogether, and the promise that the distinguished guest would be emerging shortly on his way to visit the Portreeve, managed to produce an atmosphere more appropriate to the outside of a sick room.

But as soon as this was done, Shardovan's long shadow slipped across the flagstones towards them, and his querulous voice undid the quiet. 'Why are these women here? Is this a holiday?'

It was the turn of the Castrovalvan women to turn and shush him. Tegan threw him an unfriendly glance, which he did not deign to acknowledge, and ducked back into the Doctor's room.

Between them Mergrave and Ruther explained to Shardovan that the Doctor's health was failing, and arrangements had been made to carry him to the Portreeve. The Librarian greeted the news with scarcely veiled amusement—not, he hastened to point out, on account of the Doctor's illness, which was of course a serious burden to them all, but because of the unusual idea the strangers had brought with them of carrying a man around in a box. 'I wonder,' Shardovan speculated, 'whether this new fashion will replace hunting?'

As if on cue, the door opened, and Tegan and Nyssa emerged carrying the Zero Cabinet. Shardovan stepped briskly forward, offering to help.

'No! Keep away from him,' Tegan cried, rather more loudly than she intended. And for the first time she saw the lofty keeper of the books betray signs of embarrassment. 'Please, ma'am,' he said in an altogether more human voice, 'I insist I do my small part.'

He took one of the front corners of the Zero Cabinet. Tegan was carrying the other, so it was hard to ignore his tall, dark presence as they proceeded across the terrace and along the covered walk. Ruther and Mergrave, supporting the other end of the Cabinet, could be heard tutting and gossiping among themselves, but the women, who had formed an impromptu vanguard to the little procession, maintained a respectful silence, and some even walked with their heads bowed.

Tegan suddenly realised from odd words caught from the two

bearers at the rear, and from the censorious glances she received whenever she looked across at Shardovan, that she was expected to join the group of women trailing behind. Luckily Nyssa sensed her predicament and ran forward to give her moral support, ousting Shardovan from his position with aristocratic tact and taking one corner herself. Shardovan yielded with surprising good grace and fell behind, though not so far behind as to have to walk with the women.

So they processed, over umber flagstones, past walls where apricot trees ripened in the sun. And then there were steps curving down to a lower terrace. Here the two girls had to hold back the weight of the Zero Cabinet as they descended, and at the same time struggle to keep their dignity under the aloof gaze of Shardovan.

At the bottom of the steps cries and much waving of arms from the women behind directed them through an arch into a terraced garden where the breeze drew a strong clean savoury perfume from a profusion of small white flowers. Further on, the path was banked on either side by dark box hedges of an impermeable density. Other paths led off at intervals—it was very like a maze— and one of the women had to run ahead to show Tegan and Nyssa the way.

They did not realise it at the time, but it was hereabouts that they lost Shardovan. He had eventually fallen back behind the women, a solitary, moody figure, only dubiously still attached to the procession. At one junction he halted, his eye caught by something at the bend of one of the subsidiary walks that trickled away from the central path. A hand seemed to sprout from the thick wall of the hedge—and it was beckoning to him.

Shardovan hesitated as the procession walked on around a corner. He looked again towards the mysterious hand; it beckoned once more . . . and then disappeared. Shardovan turned from the path the others had taken and went to investigate.

The thick green hedges opened on either side into an Italian garden, a circular pillared walk in the centre of which stood a mossy bust to some long-forgotten dignitary. It was the perfect place for a tryst, but even the most clandestine of meetings requires a minimum of two participants. The dignitary being devoid of limbs of any kind, Shardovan looked elsewhere around the empty garden for the owner of the beckoning finger.

It found him before he found it. The hand snaked from behind the pillar he was leaning against and clamped itself over his mouth. A voice he almost recognised said: 'Sssh!' and Shardovan turned to confront his assailant.

It was the Doctor.

The curious route the women had chosen now brought the procession out into the inevitable town square. On the far side a broad flight of granite steps that sagged under the weight of centuries of wear led the way down towards an avenue of pollarded trees. In descending Tegan glimpsed a tiny monster darting across her path, and then suddenly there was a shoal of them, as if the grey fleckled granite had decided to come alive beneath her feet.

Before she had time to realise they were harmless lizards she missed her footing on the uneven surface, and in stumbling almost dropped her corner of the Doctor. But Nyssa managed to take the weight in time, and Tegan got back into step without any mishap. 'I wish he'd levitate again,' she whispered to Nyssa. 'He's so heavy.'

They went on a pace or two, and then Nyssa leaned across to her and said something in reply that she didn't catch at first hearing. Then it finally sunk in. 'Not the Doctor! . . .' she whispered, glancing back at the Zero Cabinet. 'Then what is in there . . .?'

'*The Condensed Chronicle of Castrovalva,*' replied Nyssa with a little hide-and-seek smile. 'All thirty volumes!'

Even at the best of times the Doctor was not endowed with more than normal physical strength, but he had picked up an anatomical trick or two in the course of his travels. His grip on Shardovan's neck was light and completely painless . . . as long as his captive remained still. When he had made sure that none of the other Castrovalvans had followed, either as bodyguards or snoopers, the Doctor released his hold.

'And what, sir, do you want?' the Librarian enquired grittily, adjusting his cravat. 'Apart from the manners of a gentleman?'

'You, Shardovan,' replied the Doctor. 'You're the man I want.'

Shardovan met the Doctor's level challenging gaze. 'You will have to explain yourself, sir.'

'I think you and I understand one another.' The Doctor slipped a handkerchief from his sleeve and mopped his brow—he seemed to be in a high fever. 'You're not what you seem, my bookish friend. I suspected it when you were the only person in Castrovalva who couldn't be persuaded to join the hunting ritual.'

'My indolence would not permit it.'

'Your intelligence would not permit it! You had already guessed the whole tradition was an invention from beginning to end.' The Doctor had exchanged the handkerchief for a piece of paper, which he now handed to Shardovan. 'The proof. Your annotations of the *Condensed Chronicle*.'

Shardovan shook his head. 'Mere fancies . . . notes, sir, for a fiction I have a mind to write.'

'A civilisation evolving out of tribal warfare into a single idyllic township! It is a fiction. And the thing that clinches it . . .' The Doctor's voice had become excited, but now it broke off. He stared with the distant gaze of a man watching his departing train of thought from an empty platform.

'Well, sir?' Shardovan enquired, unmoved by the Doctor's obvious pain and embarrassment.

'I know it, I know it . . .' The Doctor was beating his forehead with his fist, willing himself to remember. 'It's on the tip of my mind . . . The books are old . . . five hundred years old at the very least. But . . .' He reeled with the effort of concentration, and had to clutch at Shardovan for support. He looked into Shardovan's eyes, as if seeking help there.

Shardovan leant him back against one of the pillars. This stranger from the world outside had so closely penetrated the secret of Castrovalva. He knew—almost. Shardovan had only to help him the last step of the way.

'The books are old,' the Librarian said quietly. 'They have been on my shelves, as you say, for half a millennium. But they chronicle the rise of Castrovalva . . . up to the present day!'

Like the sun coming out from behind a cloud the Doctor's

mind cleared. Shardovan saw the light in his eyes, and rejoiced in the understanding that passed between them. For the first time in his life Shardovan now managed to convey to a fellow being this haunting perception of a dreadful hollowness at the heart of the world.

This was done in surprisingly few words as they walked back quickly through the maze of hedges. For his part the Doctor had time to tell him of his suspicion of the cause of it all, and to explain a little about the nature of Occlusions. Shardovan's understanding of it was only shadowy. He shared with Mergrave and Ruther their blinkered view of the geography of Castrovalva—but unlike them he was at times aware of the blinkers, and aware, faintly, of a world beyond them.

They came to the garden of white flowers the procession had passed through, and Shardovan paused, as if to smell their heavy scent on the air.

'Don't tell me you're lost too?' the Doctor asked.

Shardovan shook his head. 'No, as you've guessed, Doctor, we people of Castrovalva are too much part of this thing you call the Occlusion.'

'But you do see it? The spatial anomaly?'

'With my eyes, no. But in my philosophy . . .' He pointed to a small archway cut into the hedge. 'This way. I know a back way in.'

By this time the procession had arrived at the Portreeve's house. He greeted them in the big half-timbered room, and here the Cabinet was set down on the floor. At a sign from the Portreeve, the women and followers withdrew, leaving only Mergrave, Ruther and the two girls to share the Portreeve's sadness at the fate of his friend.

Mergrave was the first to break the silence. 'Portreeve, the visitor's strange illness has progressed beyond my powers to heal.'

'We have come for your help.' Ruther matched his friend's quiet, formal tone.

The Portreeve spread wide his hands in a gesture of humility. 'Please—not my help. This is a matter for the tapestry.'

Automatically they raised their eyes to where the great

drapery hung, dominating the end wall. It was showing a confused abstract pattern, but as they watched a picture slowly formed: half landscape, half map, a depiction of the dwellings of Castrovalva and the surrounding countryside. The Portreeve's voice continued, low and even. 'The Doctor has journeyed dangerously to honour us in Castrovalva. But look at the outcome.'

The Portreeve paused. After a moment Mergrave said, with a faint hint of impatience: 'Portreeve, should we not begin.'

'Everything is in hand,' said the wise old man soothingly. 'With this tapestry, and with patience, there is nothing one cannot achieve.' He moved slowly towards the Zero Cabinet and addressed it directly. 'Nothing, Doctor, in this world or any other. The tapestry has the power to build and hold in space whole worlds of matter. But I have contented myself with one small simple town, lying in ambush for five hundred years, waiting for this moment . . .'

The note of steel that had crept into his voice made Tegan stare hard at the Portreeve. There was something about the glitter in those eyes that gazed with infinite possessiveness down at the Zero Cabinet. The ruddy amiable face of the old man seemed to dissolve as she watched, to be replaced by an all too familiar dark countenance. Tegan caught her breath in horror as the Portreeve straightened up.

'Waiting for this moment . . .' repeated the voice, swelling with triumph. 'The final meeting of the Doctor . . . and myself!'

Tegan's throat was too dry to utter a sound, but beside her she heard Nyssa gasp the name she dreaded: 'The Master!'

12

The Web is Broken

Streamers of ivy hung from the trellis over their heads, and grew so thickly in places that the greasy dark green leaves blotted out the sky. The Doctor found himself following Shardovan through sombre tunnels of foliage, until they came at last to a narrow alleyway that ran along the back of a high wall. At the end of it Shardovan held up a hand, but the command to stop was hardly necessary, for the wall now enfolded them on three sides, and there was nowhere to go except back.

Or so the Doctor thought at first. But following Shardovan's gaze led his eye towards a large circular window set high up in the wall. As he turned to look up at it, the giddiness returned, and the wall and its flounces of ivy seemed to tilt towards him, sending him reeling.

Shardovan caught him and steadied him. 'Sorry,' said the Doctor, in something like his normal voice. 'We're very close to whatever he's using to power all this. I presume this is the Portreeve's house?' Shardovan nodded. 'Then we'll have to hurry. Come on, you're a good tall chap.'

And he indicated that Shardovan help him climb up to the window. There was no time for argument about who was stronger and fitter. He was the Doctor, and the Master was his particular business.

Even Nyssa's acute mind found the idea hard to grasp. So Castrovalva was a trap, set by the Master. 'But there is a real Castrovalva—it's mentioned in the TARDIS data bank.'

The Master chuckled. 'The boy Adric entered it there at my

command.'

'Adric!' Nyssa gasped, and Tegan ran forward. 'Where is he? What have you done with him?' 'The boy is nothing,' said the Master, and began to advance toward the Zero Cabinet. 'I want the Doctor. One last long look before I destroy him utterly.'

For a moment the hideous note of triumph in his voice made Tegan forget that the Doctor was not actually inside the Cabinet that the Master was so feverishly trying to open. She was about to try to stop him, when Nyssa caught her arm, and with her eyes indicated the tapestry.

Tegan looked up. The view of Castrovalva was dissolving, and a huge circular shape was forming in its place. At first it was just a pattern of light and shade, and then the centre of the circle began to coalesce into a face . . . a face whose features were becoming clearer second by second.

The Master was still struggling with the lid of the Cabinet, but he only had to lift his eyes to see the likeness of the Doctor emblazoned across the threads of the tapestry. It was clear now that the circular shape was a window, seen from inside, set low against the floor. The Doctor was pushing against the glass in an attempt to open it, and the tapestry was trying to warn the Master.

A sudden flash drew their eyes back to the Cabinet. The Master was standing over it with what they took to be a weapon, a dark square about the size of an exercise book that was sending down a cone of orange light onto its target. The Cabinet glowed, threw off a few smoking particles of surface dust, then sank back to its dull silver colour.

The Master appeared disappointed. He tried to open the lid again, kneeling to the job this time. 'He won't get anywhere,' whispered Nyssa. 'The interface is too strong.' But Tegan was watching Mergrave and Ruther. They had not yet noticed the tapestry, but they appeared ill at ease and restless, and might turn to look at it any minute. She ran over to them.

'You've got to stop him. He's the Master.' The two Castrovalvans that turned to look at her were not the Mergrave and the Ruther she had known. Their eyes seemed quite empty of intelligence, as if they were in a trance. Behind them the tapestry showed the Doctor about to smash the circular window with his elbow.

At the sound of breaking glass the Master paused in his labour of destruction. By some miracle he failed to glance at the tapestry; the distraction from upstairs was no more than a minor irritation, and his whole mind was on the Zero Cabinet. He flicked his fingers at Ruther and Mergrave. 'What was that? Go on! Find out!' The two men moved like automaton towards the stairs that led up to the gallery.

Shardovan had found tenuous footholds in the ivy outside. The Doctor reached down for the outstretched hand and pulled him in through the open jaws of the jagged-edged window. When Shardovan had clambered in over the litter of broken glass on the floor he turned to his companion. 'And now, Doctor?'

The Doctor raised his finger to his lips and stood stock still. His consciousness buzzed with the proximity of whatever evil thing served to source the Occlusion, but listening for danger was second nature to him, and through the mental static he heard the approaching footfalls in time to pull Shardovan back against the wall. A moment later Mergrave and Ruther arrived at the top of the stairs.

But there was nowhere to hide. The two Castrovalvans saw the broken window and turned their faces towards the shadows where the Doctor and Shardovan waited for the inevitable confrontation.

In the fleeting seconds before they found him there was time to make a few preliminary guesses about their changed behaviour. Clearly some compelling force outside themselves was controlling their movements and their minds. But the Doctor guessed—or rather hoped—that some autonomy of thought remained.

It seemed he was right, for when he deliberately stepped forward into the light the contradiction of his presence before them brought confusion to their faces. 'The Doctor!' exclaimed Mergrave in a stifled voice. As a Castrovalvan it was not the fact of a man being at the same time up here on the gallery and down in the small Cabinet below that troubled him. But, as the Doctor had been bold enough to assume, there was some memory of the bond of friendship between them. Their hesitation did not last long, but it bought precious time to think.

'Wait!' Shardovan strode out from the shadows, seized his two fellow Castrovalvans by the arms, and whispered into their ears with a passion that was quite unlike himself. 'You must not betray the Doctor!'

'Betrayal, you say,' returned Ruther in a hollow voice. 'No, Shardovan. It is he who has betrayed the Portreeve.'

Shardovan's grip on them tightened and he drew them conspiratorially close. 'My dear fellow creatures. It is we who are betrayed.'

From the chamber below an enfuriated banging sound arose, but the Doctor had no time to investigate this new development. He closed with Mergrave and Ruther, determined with powerful positive thoughts of his own to oust whatever hypnotic suggestion entraced them. 'Listen carefully. This man you know as the Portreeve is the most evil force in the universe. You've got to help me defeat him. Got to, do you understand?'

As if their heads were each worked by the same wire, Ruther and Mergrave turned their pale and puzzled faces towards him, making no attempt to shake themselves free from Shardovan's grip. Their silence, emphasised by the now thunderous hammering from the ground floor, seemed to suspend the passage of time. But the Doctor knew that time was a commodity in very short supply. 'Well, say something, please,' he suggested, as politely as the urgency of the moment would permit. '"Yes", would be best.'

On the floor below the Master had abandoned technology and was belaying the Zero Cabinet with a huge poker seized from the over-sized fireplace. Nyssa and Tegan had dared to step closer to him, hoping by their silent presence to stir him on to greater fury. Anything to buy the Doctor more time.

'Something is protecting the Doctor,' the Master shouted, without pausing in his assault upon the Cabinet. 'But I will not be deterred.'

'Don't you understand anything about Zero structures?' Nyssa taunted. 'The internal interfaces are bonded by strong force interaction. The surfaces can only be separated from inside the Cabinet.'

The Master paused with the great poker held high above his head. The Doctor's face had become frozen in close-up across the expanse of the tapestry, yet still the Master failed to see it. Tegan prayed that his obsession with the Zero Cabinet would last a little longer. 'I have the Doctor in my power absolutely. But I will see his face for one last time before I destroy him forever!'

Mergrave and Ruther were returning down the stairs. The Master brought the poker down again, then, sensing the two Castrovalvans crossing the chamber towards him, said: 'Well? Speak! I gave you tongues.'

Mergrave answered in a tone of great puzzlement, as though he hardly knew what he was saying. 'You are not the Portreeve.'

The Master lowered the poker. With a sudden movement his hand snaked out and he seized the physician by the throat, pulling him close and peering into his eyes. 'Someone has been tampering with your perception threshold.'

But then Ruther spoke. 'You are not the Portreeve.'

The Master wheeled round. 'You too, Ruther? Why?'

'I believe the visitor,' said Ruther with quiet conviction. And he turned and pointed a firm straight finger towards the tapestry.

The Master froze where he stood, and the great poker slipped from his fingers, clattering onto the flagstones. And he reached down and picked up the improvised chrysalis that had carried the Doctor all the way to Castrovalva, lifted it with a great inrushing gasp of breath and held it teeteringly high above his head. 'A trick! The Doctor's here, here in the Cabinet!'

From somewhere up in the half-timbered roof came a voice that Tegan and Nyssa recognised instantly. 'Are you sure of that Master?'

The speech was gentle, but as the Master turned to confront the face on the tapestry that seemed in its silence and immobility to be mocking him, the Doctor's voice came again, an echo among the rafters. 'Are you perfectly sure?'

'Enough of your deceptions!' the Master screamed back, and with superhuman strength he hurled the Zero Cabinet across the chamber.

At the end of its arc it caught the surface of the tapestry.

Tegan held her breath, having to remind herself again that wherever the Doctor was, he was not in the Cabinet. She expected the sound of rending cloth, but instead a savage scintillation illuminated the room. The Cabinet seemed suspended in space for a moment, almost as if it were part of the tapestry's design. And then it slid down and crashed to the floor. With a sound like thunder it shattered, scattering the thirty volumes of the *Condensed Chronicle of Castrovalva* across the flagstones.

The Master looked with loathing at the scorched jumble of books. 'Where are you, Doctor. I can fetch you out, wherever you are.'

Nyssa clutched at Tegan's arm. Veils of dust were slowly cascading from the tapestry, as if the years of its history were being shed. The pattern faded, and the threads themselves seemed to be taking on a faint translucency.

Tegan put a hand to her face, suppressing a cry. Behind the tapestry, visible at first as no more than an outline, was a figure seemingly suspended in the air, its arms and legs stretched out like the spokes of a wheel. Nyssa and Tegan rushed forward, but the Doctor had already run down the sweeping staircase, and now managed to reach the tapestry ahead of them.

Tegan uttered a shrill scream, whether at the sudden shock of seeing the Doctor again, or because of a dawning recognition of the splayed imprisoned figure, she could not have said. The Doctor shouted to her to stay back, and began to pull at the tapestry. Dust fell in cataracts now, and the fabric peeled away in long shreds of rotten material.

Behind it was Adric, impaled in the centre of the glittering web.

Tegan's instinct was to run to the boy, but the Doctor grabbed her by the shoulders. 'Don't touch him, whatever you do! Leave this to me.' There was a high colour in his face, and Tegan guessed that the same bio-chemical reaction that had temporarily restored him during the crisis in the TARDIS was at work in him again. There was no telling how long it would last though. He seemed unsteady on his feet, even as he turned to confront the Master. 'So that's how you're sustaining Castrovalva!'

The Master's laughter rolled out across the chamber. 'My own adaptation of Block Transfer Computation. Since we last met, Adric's mathematical powers have been put to lively use.'

'Deadly, you mean,' said the Doctor acidly.

The Master bowed his head to acknowledge the compliment. 'That too. You were wise to deter your young friends from approaching—those Hadron power lines are lethal to the touch.' He came towards them with the easy confidence of one who holds the trump card, for his eye was on Adric, the power-less victim of the cruel mesh that only he controlled.

His overweening arrogance was chilling, but oddly it gave Nyssa the faintest grounds for hope. For arrogance is a kind of blindness, and evil that is less than perfect can be foiled. She had seen it happen often in the great days of the Traken Union.

The Doctor in his centuries of wisdom knew this too, knew it in his blood, and hoped that the Master's short-sighted vision, which now focused greedily on himself as the prize for all these centuries of waiting, would not notice Ruther behind him stooping stealthily to pick up the fallen poker.

'All right, Master,' said the Doctor, stepping forward to meet him. 'It's me you want. Let the boy go.' Ruther had the poker now, and was approaching silently out of the Master's line of sight.

'Yes, the trap is sprung,' crowed the Master, moving towards a small panel now revealed at the base of the web. 'We can begin to dispose of all the bait.'

Tegan realised he meant Adric, and caught her breath. The slight sound must have distracted the Master, for he turned his head, and this enabled him to see, out of the corner of his eye, Ruther running towards him across the flagstones with the poker held high. In an instant his black-gloved hand was at the panel, and even as the poker began its swift flight downwards towards his head, the Master slammed his finger against one of the buttons. With a hollow sucking sound, like liquid vanishing into a funnel, the determined, precise figure of Ruther became empty air, and was gone.

The Doctor did not attempt to disguise his revulsion. 'There was no need for that.'

The Master's answer was a sneer. 'I populated Castrovalva. I will dispose of these creatures as I choose.' And he threw a meaningful glance towards Mergrave.

Nyssa chose that moment to touch Tegan's hand. While all eyes had been on Ruther she had noticed Shardovan looking down from the gallery, and watched him as he climbed over the balustrade onto the long beam that ran the length of the room. Tegan followed her companion's gaze and saw the Librarian walking towards the tapestry on his precarious perch.

The Doctor was matching the Master's commandeering tone with his own particular brand of defiance. 'They may be the by-product of your evil invention, Master. But they are people. They have their own will, like Adric. Unless you let every one of them go free . . . now . . .'

'Yes, Doctor?' enquired the Master, knowing full well the Doctor had no bargaining power.

Up until this minute all the Doctor's concentration had been focused on facing up to the Master, and trying to conceal the erosion of his mind that was now being accelerated by the proximity of the web in its raw state. But the tall dark-garbed figure of Shardovan on the beam above had begun to move quickly, recklessly along the beam, and the movement was impossible to miss.

The Doctor caught sight of him, and looking up, shouted: 'Shardovan, get back!'

The Master craned his neck towards the beam. Shardovan was running now, so fast it seemed impossible he should not at any minute miss his foothold and fall to the flagstones below. Only some powerful intention kept him in balance, and the Master was the first to guess what it was. He cried out: 'Don't touch the web. It's holding Castrovalva in balance. No! You do not have the will!'

'You made us, Man of Evil,' the Librarian shouted back. 'But we are free . . .' These were his last words. With deadly deliberation, Shardovan dived from the beam straight into the glittering filligree that held Adric prisoner.

Streaks of brilliant steel-blue sparks exploded into the room. Over the deafening sizzle of the depleting voltages the Master's voice rose to a shriek. 'No! The web! My web!'

He crossed his arms to protect his face, backing away from the pyrotechnics. The Doctor knew as well as his evil adversary the dangers of radiation from the Hadron power lines but his thought was for Adric. Shouting to the two girls to stay back, he ran headlong into the smouldering wreckage of the web, disappearing into a storm of sparks and smoke.

The Master shoved Tegan, Nyssa and Mergrave aside and ran to the opposite side of the room. Tegan's main concern was for the Doctor, but the wall where the tapestry had been was completely obscured by smoke, and there was nothing to see. She turned to watch the Master, and was greeted by the extraordinary sight of him climbing into the fireplace and pulling down a sort of iron grid concealed in the chimney, closing himself off from the room.

'He's mad!' she exclaimed under her breath. 'What's he doing?'

But she knew the answer even before Nyssa replied, for the fireplace began to shimmer and become translucent. 'Escaping,' said Nyssa. 'It's his TARDIS.' They did not wait to watch it vanish completely, for there was a shout from the Doctor, and the billows of smoke parted to reveal him carrying the limp body of Adric in his arms. Tegan and Nyssa ran to him.

The Doctor put the boy down in a corner away from the smoke. 'Is he all right,' Tegan asked. The Doctor shrugged. 'We'll have to see.'

'And Shardovan?' Nyssa wanted to know.

'He gave his life to help us,' the Doctor said simply. Tegan looked across to where the fireplace had been, and now nothing but a blank wall remained. 'The Master's escaped.'

'So must we,' said the Doctor grimly. 'Without that web local space will begin to fold up infinitely into itself. Come on.'

He gathered up Adric in his arms, and indicated to Tegan that she should take care of Mergrave, who was standing alone and dazed in the residue of the settling smoke. As the five of them headed for the door the selfish idea crossed Tegan's mind that Adric was going to be enough of a liability, without adding the burden of responsibility for Mergrave. She was able to dismiss it as quickly as it entered her head, but it wasn't until they had stepped out onto the terrace that she realised how very shortsighted the thought had been.

She looked again and rubbed her eyes. The geography that had been insidiously deceptive before was now blindingly baffling. A shuffled mosaic of the Castrovalva they knew, fractured into tiny shards of space, scintillated in front of their eyes. This was not some confused picture, a viewer screen gone wrong, the image in a mirror pummelled into fragments—it was the very space they occupied.

'How do we get anywhere in all this?' cried Nyssa. Even the Doctor sounded alarmed when he said: 'Stay close together. There must be a way to get back to the TARDIS.' But Mergrave was a Castrovalvan, and he could see. Without saying a word he reached out his hands for Nyssa, Tegan and the Doctor and began to move into the mêlée of scrambled space.

Whether it was in hours or merely seconds it was hard to say, for time itself seemed to have joined in the mad dance of the dimensions, but at last they came to an archway from which steps ascended at a ludicrous angle. Mergrave pointed along them. 'This way.' It seemed to Tegan that, as they climbed, the steps rotated beneath them until their feet were higher than their heads. This fragment of architecture was like some great stair-case that arched across the sky, and they were attached to the underside, mere flies walking across a ceiling. She looked down, or rather up, into a well of receding perspectives, and glimpsed on the other side of the steps the swish of white skirts as a gaggle of Castrovalvan women ran past.

Mergrave named the places he saw as they passed them, although he confessed that even to his eyes the topology of Castrovalva was becoming obscurer by the minute. They came inevitably back into the square again, and recognised fragments of the fountain.

Adric was stirring into consciousness. The Doctor sat down on the fountain's edge and put his handkerchief into the water to cool the boy's forehead. And then he stopped dead, for through the spray he could make out the entire outline of the fireplace that had dematerialised from the Portreeve's chamber.

The Doctor whistled softly. 'The Master's TARDIS! He couldn't take off! Space is squeezing in too fast.'

'Then we're all trapped,' Nyssa exclaimed.

The Doctor shook his head. 'It can't collapse without creating a breach somewhere. All we have to do is keep our eyes open, and hope we spot it when it happens.' When he said 'we' the

Doctor really meant Mergrave, for his own eyes now registered nothing but postage-stamp-sized pieces of space, turning and whirling all around him.

Mergrave's reply was not reassuring. 'Forgive me, Doctor. There is nothing but confusion in my eyes now.'

But just then the Doctor felt a stirring beside him. Adric sat up, and then stood confidently on the fountain edge surveying the square through blinking eyes. 'It's all right,' said the boy. 'I can see!'

'Of course,' cried the Doctor, jumping to his feet. 'Adric created it! Which way, Adric?'

'What am I looking for, Doctor?'

'Anything you don't recognise as Castrovalva,' said the Doctor. 'It should start to break up any minute, and when it does . . .' But even before he could finish, a great rumbling shook the ground. It was terrifying, an earthquake and a sky-quake combined, as the broken fragments of Castrovalva rattled like loose pennies in a jar and began to tumble in upon them.

But suddenly Adric was pointing and shouting. 'There, Doctor, there!' To his eyes the town square was splitting down the middle, as if being torn apart by giant hands. And in the centre of the earth's dark turmoil was a distant patch of placid, tree-fringed sky, the hillside beyond Castrovalva.

At the Doctor's crisp command they ran towards it, Adric, Mergrave, Nyssa, Tegan and the Doctor himself, hanging onto each other's hands to keep together. They heard a shrill cry behind them and glanced back to see the Master following on their heels, pursued by a raging crowd of wild Castrovalvan faces.

Mergrave let go of the Doctor's hand and fell back. 'Mergrave! What are you doing?' The Doctor had to shout, for the rumbling noise had become tumultuous.

'Goodbye, Doctor!' shouted Mergrave, turning to join his fellow Castrovalvans as they surged around the Master. The Doctor hesitated, but Adric was pulling at his hand, urging him out into the daylight that lay beyond the fast-crumbling tunnel-mouth. 'Doctor! Quickly—before it closes again.'

Nyssa and Tegan had already tumbled out into the long cool grass at the foot of the huge hill on which Castrovalva stood. 'Doctor! Adric! Please, hurry!' Tegan shouted. Above them they could see the diminished figures of their two companions standing at the heaving mouth of the tunnel, and couldn't understand why they didn't turn and jump before the earth engulfed them.

The Doctor took no pleasure in that last glimpse of his hated enemy, the Master. It was easy to forget that this despicable monster, now victim of his own trap, had been born all those centuries ago in the full dignity of Time Lordliness. Now all his strength and all his ingenuity could not inch him one step nearer the closing cave mouth, or free him from the grabbing Castrovalvans who were his own creation. The forest of flailing arms, now black from the boiling, heaving earth, pulled at him, tearing at his flesh and dragging him back into the rapidly fragmenting vista of the evil town he had dreamed into reality.

A sudden lurch of the earth sent the Doctor and Adric tumbling down towards the two girls on the grass below. A blinding wind blew in their eyes, tearing down the foliage around them. Then came a deep stillness. They stood up and looked around. The void in the hillside had closed invisibly. They raised their eyes to the hilltop where flags had fluttered on the white turrets, but there was nothing above the vegetation line but the skeletons of a few desolate bushes.

Only the total quiet, the absence of birdsong, as if the planet were in mourning for its lost town, served to remind them Castrovalva had ever existed.

'So it's gone,' said Nyssa when they came to the edge of the wood. 'Gone forever.'

'And the Master?' Adric asked.

'Let's hope so,' replied the Doctor, barely suppressing a shudder. And then, taking a deep breath and lifting his face towards the sunshine he began to run. 'One, two . . . One, two . . . Keep up there.'

The Doctor and his companions kept it up in fact all the way back to the grassy knoll above the stream where the TARDIS still stood, jammed at an angle into the ground. They emerged from the bushes, mud-bespattered and weary after their long trek, but with their lungs filled with good clean air.

'All right, rest,' the Doctor called out rather officiously, bending his knees and stretching. 'Deep breaths, everybody.' Adric, who was still a little pallid after his long ordeal, threw himself down on the grass and stared up with gratitude at the open blue sky. 'Well done, Adric,' said the Doctor. 'Nothing like a good run to clear away the—er—cobwebs, eh?'

'Why couldn't we just have walked?' asked Tegan.

The Doctor winked. 'You've got to be fit to crew the TARDIS. A trim time-ship and a ship-shape team.' He tailed off, catching sight of the lop-sided vehicle for the first time. He walked over towards it and leant over at an angle to size it up. 'Who exactly landed this?'

'I did, Doctor,' Tegan confessed. Personally she was proud of the landing, but she could see that from the Doctor's somewhat tilted point of view, it was less than perfect. All the Doctor said was: 'Hmmm . . .' which left her guessing about his mood as they all followed him in thoughtful silence towards the ship.

He held the door open, and they trooped inside one by one. Tegan was the last to go through, and the Doctor said quietly to her, with a very wicked grin: 'Do you mind if I drive?' He hadn't the heart to explain to her yet that she had never really flown the TARDIS at all—that the whole of the voyage to Castrovalva had been pre-programmed by the evil mind of the Master, who never left anything to chance.

The blue doors closed, and with a familiar chuffing sound the TARDIS grew pale, and then translucent, and was gone. The mound of grass where it had stood was left with only the faintest impression of its shape, and as the chuffing died away into the cosmic distance the first birds began to sing once more.

DOCTOR WHO

0426114558	**TERRANCE DICKS** **Doctor Who and The** **Abominable Snowmen**	£1.35
0426200373	**Doctor Who and The** **Android Invasion**	£1.25
0426201086	**Doctor Who and The** **Androids of Tara**	£1.25
0426116313	**IAN MARTER** **Doctor Who and The** **Ark in Space**	£1.25
0426201043	**TERRANCE DICKS** **Doctor Who and The** **Armageddon Factor**	£1.25
0426112954	**Doctor Who and The** **Auton Invasion**	£1.50
0426116747	**Doctor Who and The** **Brain of Morbius**	£1.35
0426110250	**Doctor Who and The** **Carnival of Monsters**	£1.25
042611471X	**MALCOLM HULKE** **Doctor Who and** **The Cave Monsters**	£1.50
0426117034	**TERRANCE DICKS** **Doctor Who and The** **Claws of Axos**	£1.35
042620123X	**DAVID FISHER** **Doctor Who and The** **Creature from the Pit**	£1.25
0426113160	**DAVID WHITAKER** **Doctor Who and The Crusaders**	£1.50
0426200616	**BRIAN HAYLES** **Doctor Who and The Curse** **of Peladon**	£1.50
0426114639	**GERRY DAVIS** **Doctor Who and The Cybermen**	£1.50
0426113322	**BARRY LETTS** **Doctor Who and The Daemons**	£1.50

Prices are subject to alteration

DOCTOR WHO

0426101103	DAVID WHITAKER **Doctor Who and The** **Daleks**	£1.50
042611244X	TERRANCE DICKS **Doctor Who and The Dalek** **Invasion of Earth**	£1.25
0426103807	**Doctor Who and The Day** **of the Daleks**	£1.35
042620042X	**Doctor Who – Death to** **the Daleks**	£1.35
0426119657	**Doctor Who and The** **Deadly Assassin**	£1.25
0426200969	**Doctor Who and The** **Destiny of the Daleks**	£1.35
0426108744	MALCOLM HULKE **Doctor Who and The** **Dinosaur Invasion**	£1.35
0426103726	**Doctor Who and** **The Doomsday Weapon**	£1.35
0426201464	IAN MARTER **Doctor Who and The** **Enemy of the World**	£1.25
0426200063	TERRANCE DICKS **Doctor Who and The** **Face of Evil**	£1.25
0426201507	ANDREW SMITH **Doctor Who – Full Circle**	£1.35
0426112601	TERRANCE DICKS **Doctor Who and The** **Genesis of the Daleks**	£1.35
0426112792	**Doctor Who and The Giant Robot**	£1.25
0426115430	MALCOLM HULKE **Doctor Who and The** **Green Death**	£1.35

Prices are subject to alteration

DOCTOR WHO

0426200330	TERRANCE DICKS Doctor Who and The Hand of Fear	£1.25
0426201310	Doctor Who and The Horns of Nimon	£1.25
0426200098	Doctor Who and The Horror of Fang Rock	£1.25
0426108663	BRIAN HAYLES Doctor Who and The Ice Warriors	£1.35
0426200772	Doctor Who and The Image of the Fendahl	£1.25
0426200934	TERRANCE DICKS Doctor Who and The Invasion of Time	£1.35
0426200543	Doctor Who and The Invisible Enemy	£1.25
0426201485	Doctor Who and The Keeper of Traken	£1.35
0426201256	PHILIP HINCHCLIFFE Doctor Who and The Keys of Marinus	£1.35
0426201477	DAVID FISHER Doctor Who and The Leisure Hive	£1.25
0426110412	TERRANCE DICKS Doctor Who and The Loch Ness Monster	£1.25
0426201493	CHRISTOPHER H BIDMEAD Doctor Who – Logopolis	£1.25
0426118936	PHILIP HINCHCLIFFE Doctor Who and The Masque of Mandragora	£1.25
0426201329	TERRANCE DICKS Doctor Who and The Monster of Peladon	£1.25

Prices are subject to alteration

STAR Books are obtainable from many booksellers and newsagents. If you have any difficulty please send purchase price plus postage on the scale below to:-

Star Cash Sales
P.O. Box 11
Falmouth
Cornwall
OR
Star Book Service,
G.P.O. Box 29,
Douglas,
Isle of Man,
British Isles.

While every effort is made to keep prices low, it is sometimes necessary to increase prices at short notice. Star Books reserve the right to show new retail prices on covers which may differ from those advertised in the text or elsewhere.

Postage and Packing Rate
UK: 45p for the first book, 20p for the second book and 14p for each additional book ordered to a maximum charge of £1.63. BFPO and EIRE: 45p for the first book, 20p for the second book, 14p per copy for the next 7 books thereafter 8p per book. Overseas: 75p for the first book and 21p per copy for each additional book.